"It's over. I only waited until you were awake so that I could say goodbye."

"G-goodbye! This isn't funny, Ronan!"

"Funny?" His intonation said it all. "This is no joke, my darling. No joke at all. Our marriage, such as it was, is over—done with. I'm leaving today and I'm never coming back."

KATE WALKER was born in Nottinghamshire, England, but since she grew up in Yorkshire she has always felt that her roots are there. She met her husband at university and she originally worked as a children's librarian, but after the birth of her son she returned to her old childhood love of writing. When she's not working, she divides her time between her family, their three cats and her interests of embroidery, antiques, film and theater and, of course, reading.

Wife for a Day

KATE WALKER

SWEET REVENGE

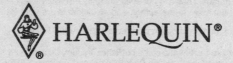

HARLEQUIN®

TORONTO • NEW YORK • LONDON
AMSTERDAM • PARIS • SYDNEY • HAMBURG
STOCKHOLM • ATHENS • TOKYO • MILAN • MADRID
PRAGUE • WARSAW • BUDAPEST • AUCKLAND

ISBN 0-373-80547-0

WIFE FOR A DAY

First North American Publication 2002.

This edition published by arrangement with Harlequin Books S.A.

® and TM are trademarks of the publisher. Trademarks indicated with
® are registered in the United States Patent and Trademark Office, the
Canadian Trade Marks Office and in other countries.

Visit us at www.eHarlequin.com

Printed in U.S.A.

CHAPTER ONE

RONAN GUERIN looked down at the sleeping face of the woman in the bed and almost changed his mind about the whole thing.

Almost.

She looked so peaceful, so innocent, so damned beautiful. It was impossible not to recall the night he had just spent with her, the incandescent passion they had shared, and feel a pang of regret for the course he had started out on.

But then he remembered Rosalie, every bit as beautiful and just as innocent, and he hardened his heart. Firming his resolve, he reached out a hand and touched her shoulder gently.

'Lily...' he said softly.

At first there was no response. She was too deeply unconscious, too exhausted by a night in which sleep had been the last thing on their minds to hear. Refusing to let himself reconsider, to be weakened by the sight of her innocent appearance, he shook her slightly, watching as she gave a faint murmur and stirred, her eyes still closed.

'Good morning, wife.'

Good morning, wife. The words reached Lily through the clouds of sleep that clogged her brain, making them sound vague and indistinct so that she frowned in drowsy confusion.

Wife?

It was as she moved languorously in the deep comfort of the bed, feeling the soft brush of the fine linen sheets on her naked body, that realisation struck home with the force of an arrow thudding straight into the heart of a target. Her eyes, wide and deep gold, flew open, meeting the steady, watchful gaze of the man who sat on the edge of the bed, his strong fingers still resting on her arm.

'Ronan?'

Of course! How could she have forgotten, even for a second? How could sleep have wiped away the fact that this was the man

5

to whom she had given her heart so completely that there was never a hope of getting it back—not that she wanted it. The man who, only the day before, had placed a gold wedding band on her finger as he vowed to love and honour her for the rest of his life.

Stretching luxuriously, she turned to face him.

'Good morning, husband.'

Her smile, with its deliberate edge of sleepy sensuality, was directed straight into his intent blue-grey eyes, the angle of her head calculatedly provocative as it splayed the long blonde strands of her hair out around her heart-shaped face on the immaculate white pillows.

To her surprise, neither the smile nor the inviting gesture earned her the response she had anticipated. Instead, Ronan seemed strangely, almost worryingly distant. The strong-boned features under the silky dark chestnut hair were set in a way that made him look disturbingly remote and cold, light-years away from the ardent, passionate lover of the night before.

Memories of the indulgence of that night brought a rush of colour to her cheeks, and her tongue slipped out to smooth over the soft curve of her lower lip, as if she could still taste the burning kisses he had pressed there. A hot rush of sexual awareness mixed with a heady sense of very female triumph flooded every nerve as she saw the indigo gaze drop to follow the slight movement.

'Husband,' she murmured again, savouring the sound of the word.

Her body still ached faintly, and there were one or two tender spots on her skin, but she didn't care. The pleasure she had experienced last night had been so totally new to her, so mind-blowing in its intensity, that she had been hard put to it to believe that she could feel it and not shatter into a thousand tiny pieces.

And it was something she very much wanted to enjoy all over again.

As she believed Ronan would too. In fact, when she had finally drifted into exhausted and satiated sleep, she had been convinced that she would wake to find herself firmly enclosed by the strength of his arms. That he would greet her with gentle kisses, rouse her body to demanding life, as he had done so easily the night before, his own muscular frame heating, tensing, hardening in matching response.

Which was why it was so disconcerting to find him now sitting beside her, looking so cool and indifferent—and fully dressed.

'What time is it?' she asked in some concern, recalling the flight they were due to make that day.

'Just after nine.'

'So early! Then what are you doing out of bed?'

Her full mouth formed a petulant moue of disapproval as she took in the clothes he was wearing. They were hardly suitable for someone about to set out on a long-haul trip to the tropical island he had promised would be their honeymoon destination. The immaculately tailored suit in a light grey silk, white shirt and conservative tie only added to her confusion, aggravating the sense of alienation she had experienced earlier.

'Our plane doesn't leave until three!' she protested. 'We've hours yet.'

Lily reached out and stroked his hand where it lay, broad and strong, with long, square-tipped fingers, on the pristine whiteness of the quilt cover.

'Come back to bed,' she murmured, her low voice pitched to entice.

An adamant shake of his gleaming dark auburn head was Ronan's only response. His disturbingly shadowed gaze was fixed on the thick gold band that gleamed bright and new on her slender finger.

'No?'

Incredulity sharpened her voice, giving a disbelieving lift to the single syllable. Was this the same man who had been so physically demanding, so insatiable throughout the night? The same Ronan as the one who had allowed her no rest until they were both limp with exhaustion, unable to move, even to breathe properly?

'What is it, darling?' Deliberately she lowered her voice to a husky whisper. 'Have you gone off me already?'

That got a reaction, but not the one she had expected.

With a jerky movement, Ronan lifted his head so that his eyes once more met hers full on. Coolest sea-blue locked with the almost amber warmth of Lily's perplexed gaze, and something deep in those eyes, some shadow darkening their limpid clearness, made her shiver in intuitive apprehension.

'Gone off you?' he echoed, his voice sounding as if it came from a throat that was painfully raw. 'Never that!'

As if to emphasise the words, he accompanied them with a look so sensually appreciative, so blatantly carnal, that it was almost a physical caress in itself. But, just as Lily was about to relax back into the comfortable warmth of her sleepy sexuality, the realisation of a cold edge to that look, a glitter of something disturbing in his eyes was like the splash of icy water in her face, bringing all her defences to red alert before he even spoke again.

'You turn me on just by existing, lady,' he declared with disturbing harshness. 'And you know it. I only have to look at you to want you so much that I feel I might die if I don't have you. But that's a penance I have to endure.'

'Penance!'

That first tiny prickle of unease had now become a raging tide of discomfort. Every nerve stung with a tension that was like the pins and needles of blood returning to a numbed limb, but magnified a hundredfold.

'I don't understand!'

She couldn't hide the tremor of her voice as she pushed herself upright in a panic, feeling far too vulnerable lying down.

'Ronan? What is it?'

'I want you, Lily,' Ronan persisted, as if she hadn't spoken. Each word was so cold, so clipped that Lily flinched away from them as if they were actually formed in ice as they fell on the sensitive skin of her exposed neck and shoulders. 'But I'll never have you again—ever. It was good while it lasted—perhaps the best—but now it's over. I only waited until you were awake so that I could say goodbye.'

'G-Goodbye!'

It couldn't be true! She couldn't have heard right. Either that or this was some appalling sick joke, one that she didn't like at all. But she would never have believed that Ronan could be so hatefully cruel.

'This isn't funny, Ronan!'

'Funny?'

His intonation said it all, Ronan knew. There was no need for further elucidation. But still he wanted to spell it out to her, setting out the details with a precise pedantry that made it plain his intent was to spare her nothing. He wanted her to know exactly what was happening, to understand what the experience of pain was truly like.

'This is no joke, my darling. No joke at all. Believe me, I never felt further from laughter; I couldn't be more serious. Our marriage, such as it was, is over—done with. I'm leaving today and I'm never coming back.'

He got to his feet, the easy, indolent movement somehow shocking when Lily contrasted it with the whirling frenzy inside her head.

'I'll let you decide when to serve the divorce papers.'

'But...'

'And now, if you'll excuse me...' The carefully formal politeness underlined the ruthless determination to give her no quarter at all. 'I have a long drive ahead of me.'

As he strolled to the door Lily could only stare after him in stunned confusion. But even as her golden eyes were fixed on his retreating back her thoughts were turned inward, reviewing the events of the previous day—their wedding day—trying to see how the glorious happiness she had experienced then could have brought her to the emotional horror of this moment.

How was it possible that what had seemed like the realisation of her greatest dream could have changed so swiftly into the nightmare of knowing that that fulfilment now lay shattered at her feet?

How could she not have suspected anything? Surely there must have been some clue. Some moment when Ronan had let slip the careful mask of the happy bridegroom, the veneer of a man anticipating his marriage with the same sort of excitement and delight that had filled her own heart, and revealed his true feelings.

Because it had to have been a mask, she now saw. He could never have felt for her the way she had believed he did and then turn round and do this. And yet he had never seemed to be pretending. Certainly, she had never suspected for a moment that his feelings were anything but totally sincere.

So when had it all fallen apart?

No, it couldn't be true! She had to be dreaming. She was trapped in a nightmare from which she desperately wished she could wake.

Frantically she pinched at her hand, her arm, praying that the small, self-inflicted pain would break through the trance that held her and force her into consciousness. But nothing happened. There was nothing *to* happen. She was wide awake, this private hell only too real.

And yesterday she had thought she had it all. That she'd found the true love she had looked for all her life.

Yesterday had been quite perfect. In fact the one tiny flaw she could remember had been the silly upset over Ronan's hair...

'Well, are you ready to take the longest walk of your life?'

George Halliday grinned down at Lily as he spoke, one hand adjusting the fall of his elaborate cravat. Above the silky material, his lined face was already beginning to redden in the unexpected warmth of early April sunlight.

'The longest walk, Uncle George?'

Lily smiled enquiringly up at the man who wasn't really her uncle but had acquired the name as an honorary title after years of friendship. George had held the market stall next to hers when she had first started out in her florist's business. He had been there to help when she had moved her business into a small, rented shop, and he was the closest thing to a genuine relation she had had for years. So he had been the obvious choice to turn to when, with her wedding so very close, she had been unable to track down her missing brother and had been forced to look elsewhere for someone to escort her down the aisle.

'I thought that was supposed to be the walk to the scaffold.'

'Tradition might have it that way, my dear, but I can't see it. I reckon that particular stroll must just fly by! But this one! Well, that's a different kettle of fish altogether. Too much time to think.

With every step you take you're wondering whether you've done the right thing. He loves me...he loves me not...'

He mimed slow, stately steps forward with each phrase.

'Oh, Uncle George! I don't have to think, I *know*! I love Ronan more than life itself, and he loves me.'

'Well, just so long as you're sure. If you ask me, this was all a bit of a rushed job.'

His worried frown told her exactly what he was thinking, and she hurried to put his mind at rest on that score.

'No, I'm not pregnant, if that's what you're hinting at. We haven't even slept together yet. Ronan knew I preferred to wait. He understood...'

'Then he's a rare sort of man if he did,' George declared with typical Yorkshire bluntness. 'But that explains his haste to get you down the aisle, I suppose. If I was thirty years younger, and had a beauty like you wearing my ring, then I know I'd want to rush through the wedding pretty damn quick too. Every day I had to wait would seem like an eternity.'

'Uncle George!'

Warm colour flooded Lily's face from her slender neck right up under the coils of blonde hair that were topped by a delicate crystal tiara, and she lifted her bouquet of white lilies to try to conceal her blushes.

'Now don't you go coy on me, young madam! I know you're twenty-six, and that's quite old enough to know what I mean. Your Ronan would have to be dead from the neck down if he didn't know what a treasure he's getting in you.'

'I think you can rest easy on that score,' Lily assured him, some very personal memories starting up her blushes again just as they were beginning to ebb.

Ronan might have acceded to her desire to wait until their wedding night before they slept together, but that didn't mean he had acquiesced easily, or waited with patience or restraint. They had come very close to breaking their resolution more than once in recent days, and she for one was more than thankful that theirs had been only a very short engagement. As it was, it would be barely two months from the moment they had met until their wedding day, and for Lily that was more than enough.

The sound of the organ beginning the familiar notes of the traditional 'Wedding March' brought her attention back to the present, making her turn towards the door into the church. With slightly shaky fingers she adjusted the sleek, elegant lines of her ivory silk dress, smoothing the long skirt down carefully. Then, lifting her head high, she turned a wide, confident smile in her companion's direction.

'Time to go!'

'No second thoughts?'

'None at all. You were right, Uncle George. Ronan is a very rare sort of man, and that's exactly why I'm marrying him.'

The interior of the church looked every bit as beautiful as she had imagined when she had planned the designs for the floral arrangements, with creamy old-fashioned roses at the base of the stained glass windows and white freesias, lily of the valley and trailing ivy decorating the end of every pew. On the altar, two tall displays of lilies mirrored the flowers in her bouquet, their elegant height, creamy waxen petals and golden stamens making them look very similar to the traditional church candles one might have expected to see there.

But no real candles burned anywhere inside the old building. Lily had explained her feelings on that matter when she had booked the church, and the priest had understood perfectly. So the only illumination on the altar itself came from the soft light of the early spring sun that poured through the wide, arched windows behind it.

The next moment Lily's gaze went to the man standing tall and straight before the altar, his tall frame lovingly enhanced by the perfect cut of his formal morning coat, and immediately she forgot everything else. This was Ronan, her fiancé, so soon to be her husband.

Her heart kicked sharply under the tightly boned bodice as her amber-coloured gaze drank in the power and strength of his long body, the straight line of his back and firm, square shoulders. His feet were planted firmly on the stone-flagged floor, his legs strong and steady, with no trace of the nervous tremble that had suddenly affected her own. The sun that slanted through the nearby window fell directly onto his head, making the burnished copper strands gleam amongst the silken darkness.

But that was when she noticed the change in his appearance that had made her do a double take.

His hair! Ronan had cut his beautiful hair! Where only the day before it had been thick and shining, with a strong natural wave, now the chestnut locks were clipped into an uncompromising crop that exposed the back of his tanned neck.

Lily had to bite down hard on her lower lip to hold back the small sound of disappointment that almost escaped her. She had loved to curl her fingers in that dark silk, and had looked forward to doing just that in the intimate privacy of their wedding night. Short-haired, he looked older, harder, the change in his appearance seeming to emphasise the dynamic, forceful side of his nature that had led to his reputation as a ruthless businessman but which she had rarely seen in her own dealings with him.

But she couldn't say anything about it now. Already the priest had moved forward to begin the ceremony, and at her side Ronan had turned to face her. Every other thought fled from her mind as he took her hand in the warm strength of his and she saw the blaze of appreciation that flared in his eyes as he took in her appearance fully for the first time.

In that moment it was as if the church and the congregation had melted into one multicoloured blur. There was only herself and Ronan and the promises they were making to each other, the vows of love, honour and faithfulness for the rest of their lives.

And all the time, in the depths of that intent grey-blue stare, burned the evidence of a desire so strong, so ardent that it set up sensations and responses in her own body that were entirely inappropriate to their surroundings and the solemnity of the occasion.

But once the service was over, and they were at the reception in a nearby hotel, Lily couldn't hold back disappointment any longer and she turned on Ronan reproachfully.

'You cut your hair! Why did you do that?'

'And happy wedding day to you too, my love,' was the swiftly sardonic response. Ronan's straight, dark brows drew together in a faint frown. 'What happened to, I love you, darling husband. I'm so happy to be your wife?'

Hearing an unexpected and perturbing fervour behind his words, Lily caught herself up on what she had been about to say and substituted instead a careful echoing of his own phrase.

'I love you, darling h-husband.'

To her consternation her tongue tangled round the word, turning it into a stumbling and gauche hiccup.

Was it real? Could Ronan really be her *husband*? After all the days of impatiently counting the hours, the nights of dreaming of just this moment, it seemed impossible that at last those dreams had finally come true.

'I'm so happy to be your wife.'

'*Are* you?'

It was there again, that worrying emphasis, a sharpness that edged his words with steel. His eyes were silver fire, seeming to want—to need—to drag the response from her, rooting it out of her very soul.

'*Are* you happy? Truly happy?'

'Of course I am.' Reaction to the unexpected ferocity of his questioning put a small quiver into her voice. 'Ronan, what is this, the Spanish Inquisition?'

'I just wanted to be sure.'

'Sure!'

Ronan's sudden and uncharacteristic need for reassurance sent a rush of delight and excitement through her, flooding her heart with renewed love for him. The thought that even a man as self-contained and assured as Ronan had proved himself to be could feel insecure where she was concerned spoke of such a depth of emotion that it brought hot tears to her eyes.

'Oh, Ronan, how could I not be sure? I've just married the man I love in front of all my friends. Everyone I know is here...'

'Except Davey,' Ronan inserted almost harshly.

'Except Davey,' Lily agreed solemnly.

This time the tears that stung so sharply stemmed from a very different source. It would have made her day perfect if her brother could have been there.

'I wish I'd been able to get in touch with him.'

'So do I,' said Ronan, with such feeling that Lily looked up at him in some surprise.

'I didn't know it mattered so much to you.'

'Well, let's just say that I would have preferred to have met your brother before today.'

His eyes drifted away from her to stare out across the crowded room, but Lily got the distinct impression that he saw nothing of the brightly dressed guests, laughing and chatting in small friendly groups. Slowly he drew a deep, uneven breath, and when he turned back to her his expression had altered in some subtle, indefinable way. And when he spoke again she had the strangest feeling that he was not pursuing the topic that had been uppermost in his thoughts.

'After all, we're not exactly well off for family, either of us. We're two adults of not exactly ancient years, and yet we can't muster even a single relative between us.'

'I know...'

It was a sigh of sorrow and regret as her thoughts went to her own parents, killed in a tragic accident when she had been seventeen and Davey six years younger. They would have loved to be here today, to see her as a happy bride, and she had no doubt that they would have approved of this tall, handsome, successful, but above all *loving* man she had chosen as her husband.

Sadly, Ronan, too, was on his own. When she had asked him which of his relatives she should invite to the wedding, his reply had been short to the point of curtness.

'No family. There's no family, but I can give you a list of friends if you like.'

And the number of his friends had gone a long way towards making up for the shortfall on the family side, she reflected. Not only that, but some of them had already created quite a stir in this small northern town, one that would persist long after the wedding celebrations were over. As an extremely wealthy businessman, whose extensive interests amounted to an empire, Ronan had contact with equally rich and well-known people, many of whom were here today.

Not that she had had much of an opportunity to talk to any of them. Ronan had kept her very much at his side so that she hadn't had much of a chance to get to know any of his guests. She could only hope that they wouldn't hold it against her later.

A faint frown drew Lily's fair brows together as she recalled her meeting with one of Ronan's particular friends. His best man, Connor Fitzpatrick, had seemed rather distant when she had been introduced to him the day before, and he had subjected her to a disturbingly close scrutiny that had distinctly unnerved her. Hannah, her own best friend and chief bridesmaid, was having much more success with him now on the dance floor, some remark she had made earning her a wide, brilliant smile.

'Why the black look?' Ronan had caught the change in her expression.

'I was just thinking that I get the impression Connor doesn't really like or approve of me.'

Those steely eyes flashed swiftly in the direction of his friend, that hint of a frown returning just for a moment. But then a second later Ronan turned back to her with a smile that dismissed her fears as foolish and unnecessary.

'What's not to like or approve, little silly?' he murmured softly. 'To tell you the truth, he's probably far more likely to doubt *my* own sincerity and motives in entering into this marriage. After all, I've hardly been the type to settle down until now, and, let's face it, this was something of a whirlwind romance. You knocked me right off my feet and I haven't been able to regain my balance ever since.'

Those words had reassured her at the time, Lily recalled miserably, reluctantly coming back to the present to find herself still staring at the door through which Ronan had just disappeared. But now they rang brutally hollow, overlaid instead by the cold, callous declaration that he was leaving and never coming back.

The sound of a door opening downstairs jolted her into movement. What was she doing sitting here like this, letting Ronan go? He was her husband! They'd been married for less than twenty-four hours. Was she going to let him leave without a fight?

Frantically she flung back the bedclothes, snatching up the mint-green wrap-around robe that lay on a chair beside the bed.

Refusing to allow herself to dwell on the fact that the matching silk and lace nightdress which she had worn so briefly the night before now lay in a crumpled heap on the floor, where Ronan had discarded it in the heat of his passion, she yanked it on, tugging the belt fastened as she headed for the stairs.

The front door stood wide open, letting in the sunlight and the sound of birdsong. The cheerful noise stabbed at her, bringing home the contrast between its light-hearted notes and the dark sense of dread that dulled her own soul.

'Ronan!'

He was already outside, standing by his car as he loaded his case into the boot. The sight made her heart thud against her chest in shocked recognition that he had meant what he had said. Even now, she had still held on to the weak thread of hope that it had all just been some sick, tasteless joke.

'Ronan, wait!'

He ignored her, his dark head turned away, the set of his broad shoulders under the tailored jacket seeming to declare unrelenting rejection of her plea without a word being spoken.

'Oh, please, don't do this!' She reached the steps from the main door as she spoke. 'Ronan, you can't do this to me. I won't let you!'

Slowly, deliberately, Ronan reached up and slammed the lid of the boot closed. The dull thud it made reverberated inside Lily's head, making her think fearfully of steel doors slamming in her face, or the sound of a clock sounding an hour she had dreaded.

But then he turned, and at the sight of his face all other thoughts fled from her mind, leaving it cold and hollow with dread.

This wasn't Ronan! This wasn't the man she loved with all her heart, the man she had given herself to, body and soul, only the day before!

It was as if some stranger had moved in, an alien, who had taken over Ronan's body, ejecting his spirit and leaving behind only the shell of the man to whom she had given her heart. A stranger with the same burnished hair, the same devastatingly attractive features, the same lean, strong build.

But these were not the same eyes—not her Ronan's eyes. They were cold and hard as tempered steel, lethal as a stiletto-blade, impregnable as metal shutters.

'You can't...' she began again, but her voice had lost all conviction.

The look Ronan turned on her was wintry, bleak as the coldest November day.

'I can do anything I want,' he flung at her. 'Just try and stop me.'

CHAPTER TWO

LILY did the only thing she could think of.

Heedless of the fact that she was wearing nothing but the green robe, and determinedly ignoring the bite of the gravel into the soles of her bare feet, she ran out into the drive and caught hold of the sleeve of Ronan's jacket, clinging on to it tightly.

'I won't let you go until you give me some sort of an explanation! You owe me that at least!'

The words were swallowed back down her throat as she met the inimical blaze of his glare, his eyes burning translucent in the spring sunlight. Ronan shrugged off her clinging hold with a negligence that was positively insulting.

'I owe you nothing,' he declared, fastidiously adjusting the fit of his jacket before opening the front door of his car. 'If anything, the debts are all on your side.'

'On my... Oh, no, you don't!'

Seeing that he was about to slide into the driver's seat, she lurched forward once more, this time fastening her arms around his narrow waist from behind.

She realised just how big a mistake she had made as soon as her fingers locked together above the polished metal buckle on the narrow leather belt he wore. Now her hands were resting on the taut, flat plane of his stomach, her hold bringing her breasts and hips into close contact with the firm line of his back.

She had held him like this last night, only then he had been warm and approachable, not this glacially hostile stranger. He had been wearing only a towelling robe, having got up in the middle of the night for some reason. She had woken to find him staring out of the bedroom window and had crept up behind him, coming close and sliding her arms around him just as now.

But it had been so very different then. Then she had felt his immediate response, his sudden tension, the reaction of his body betraying his hunger for her with a speed that had made her laugh out loud in delight. She had pressed up against the width of his back, sliding her fingers under the loosely tied belt of his robe, sighing her pleasure as she'd encountered the warm smoothness of his flesh.

And Ronan had sighed too, a sound that was half a gasp of pleasure, half a moan of surrender as he'd swivelled round within the confines of her arms to gather her close to him.

But under these very different circumstances such memories and the cruel stab of pain they brought were a source of weakness. If she let them they would undermine her resolve. They had already left her vulnerable to Ronan's immediate reaction, making it only too easy for him to break free from her hold with a force that sent her spinning away, crashing painfully into the side of the car.

'I'm *going,* Lily,' he declared harshly. 'And nothing you can do will stop me.'

This was proving so much harder than he had anticipated. She had only to touch him and every nerve in his body set up a clamorous demand, tightening until there was an ache in his groin that pleaded for the release of pleasure that he had known the night before.

When he had started out on this, he had believed he could keep all emotion out of it. He hadn't reckoned on wanting her so much. But he had to fight that base need. It would destroy him and leave his plan in ashes if he didn't.

It took all his strength to wrench himself away instead of turning and gathering her up in his arms, kissing her with the sort of hungry sensuality that took him with it into mindless oblivion.

Despair tore at Lily's heart as she saw him slide into the driving seat and push his key firmly into the ignition. Despair combined with the feelings that now assailed her to make it impossible to think clearly.

She had known only one night of this man's lovemaking, had spent just a few short hours in his arms, but her body knew his so intimately it was as if she was some slave of long ago, marked with her master's brand. She had only to touch him and every sense sprang into vivid, throbbing life. Each nerve burned sharply, awakening, yearning, *demanding* the pleasure his caresses could bring.

Like a finely tuned instrument responding to the skill of a master performer, she had only to feel the warmth of his body, inhale the intensely personal scent of his skin, feel his heart beating under her cheek and she was lost. Able only to perform the tune that he decided to play.

But if she didn't act *now*, and quickly, he would be gone, and she would never see him again. She didn't doubt that he meant what he said; conviction was stamped into every hard line into which his face was set. The trouble was that she had no idea why.

A sudden blaze of panic brought a desperate clarity to her thoughts. An idea so crazy it might just work sprang into her mind, pushing her into action. Not giving herself time to lose her nerve, she swung round sharply and clambered up on to the bonnet of the Mercedes, gathering her inadequate clothing around her as she did so.

'*Lily!*' It was a bellow of pure rage. 'Get off there!'

'Make me!'

Just for a second, as the engine revved fiercely, she feared he might actually call her bluff and drive off with her still perched up there. Horrific visions of the powerful car speeding down the drive, making a few wild zigzagging turns designed to throw her off, filled her head, making her blood run cold. She had just reached the point where she was actually fearfully contemplating the damage that would be the result of a fall from the fast-moving vehicle on to the gravel, when Ronan took his foot off the accelerator.

The sound of the motor died abruptly. Lily barely had time to sigh with relief before the driver's door was pushed open violently. Getting out, Ronan stalked towards her, white marks of fury etched around his nose and mouth.

'Lily...'

When he finally stood beside her, hands braced on his hips, indigo eyes blazing incandescent with anger, it took all of Lily's mental strength not to shrink back against the windscreen.

Instead she forced herself to face him with what she hoped was a look of cool defiance.

'You're not making this easy for me!' he declared through tightly clenched teeth.

'I don't want to make it *easy*! I plan on making it as difficult as possible for you to leave me, because I—'

'Are you really so desperate that you'd beg me to stay when it must be painfully clear that it's the last thing on God's earth I want to do? That I obviously can't stand the sight of you.'

'But last night...'

'Last night was last night. It was an appalling mistake—a mental aberration—and one I most definitely do not intend to let happen again.'

'It didn't feel like that to me!'

But then what experience did she have to go on? She had only had one other brief, unsatisfactory love affair, which had been more a relationship of the mind than any great physical passion. Kristian's lovemaking had been comfortable, uninspired, and totally unexciting when compared to the fires Ronan could light inside her. Fires that she had never suspected could exist, whose sheer, elemental force had rocked her world, making her feel that she had lost her grip on everything she had formerly believed herself to be.

In Ronan's arms she became another woman entirely. A wild, wanton, primitive creature, who met his passion with a hunger that matched and occasionally even outstripped it.

'You wanted it every bit as much as I did!' she flung at him. 'You—'

'Women aren't the only ones who can fake it,' Ronan shot back callously, making her thoughts reel with the cruelty of the gibe.

'Oh, now I *know* you're lying! There was nothing fake about last night—about any of it!'

If she believed that then he would have destroyed everything. All her precious memories of her wedding night. The night she had believed marked the beginning of the most wonderful part of her existence. The night she now feared would be the only experience she would ever have of married life.

She hadn't even known about the house. That had been a surprise Ronan had sprung on her at the very last moment. When she had left the reception and got into the car with him, she had believed that they were heading for the airport and a plane ride to the honeymoon destination he had kept a closely guarded secret from her.

But, 'There's been a change of plan,' he had told her as the last of the waving, cheering guests had disappeared from view. 'Our plane doesn't leave until three tomorrow afternoon.'

'Tomorrow!'

Automatically, Lily had glanced back towards the hotel they had just left, thinking of the way, only half an hour before, she had been giggling excitedly with Hannah as they'd tried to guess just where in the world Ronan planned on taking her.

'But where will we spend tonight?'

'You leave that to me.' A small, enigmatic smile had curled the corners of Ronan's wide mouth. 'I have everything under control. Just put yourself entirely in my hands and see what happens.'

Now, looking back at that moment, hearing those words again with the benefit of hindsight, Lily found that they made her shiver in spite of the warmth of the sun. Something about the way Ronan had spoken brought a sense of nausea to the pit of her stomach.

But last night, worn out by the excitement of the day, decidedly tiddly on champagne, and even more intoxicated by the thought of actually being Mrs Ronan Guerin, she had felt no such premonition of danger. Instead, she had wriggled sensuously in her seat, almost purring like a small, contented cat.

'I can't wait to *put myself in your hands*,' she'd murmured, giving the words a distinctly lascivious intonation as she ran her hand up his arm, stroking from square shoulder to strong wrist and back again. 'And I'm dying to get my hands on certain parts of you.'

This time she let her fingers slide down his jacket until they reached the strong line of his thighs. There, she walked them along the hard muscle that was stretched taut as his foot rested on the car's pedal, moving slowly and deliberately inwards, smiling as she saw it bunch in instinctive reaction.

'Behave yourself, witch!' Ronan reproved laughingly. 'You'll have us off the road if you don't stop that nonsense—Lily!' This time the warning was more serious as she ignored his protest.

'I don't want to behave!' Lily pouted with mock petulance. 'I've had to behave myself for the last eight weeks, and it's been *intensely* frustrating.'

'And whose idea was that? As I recall, you were the one who insisted on waiting until our wedding day.'

'And you agreed! But it is our wedding day now, so we don't have to wait any longer. We're legally married so I can do what I want. And I want to do this...'

Emboldened by the excitement that was building up inside her, she slid her fingers provocatively in between his thighs, her teasing smile growing wider as she heard his breath hiss sharply inwards in uncontrolled response.

'*Lily!* Be a good girl, please.'

'Oh, I'll be good.' The huskiness of her voice gave the words a very different meaning from the one he had used. 'I'll be very good. I plan to be the best you've ever known. So, wherever we're going, why don't you put your foot down? I want to get there just as fast as we possibly can.'

'Your wish is my command.'

Ronan had suited action to the words, ramming the accelerator pedal almost to the floor, and the car had sped along the road out of town, heading for the countryside.

The unexpected warmth of the day had turned into an uncomfortably close evening by the time he steered the powerful vehicle off the narrow lane and up a winding, steep drive, coming to a halt before the impressive building at the top of it.

'Wow!' Lily could only stare in amazed admiration.

Built in a stone that had been mellowed by the passage of years, the house had an elegant porch supported on Grecian-style pillars and mullioned windows that reflected the glow of the setting sun. Over half of the front was covered in luxuriant ivy that extended over the roof of the large Victorian-style conservatory attached to one side. On the other side was a formal rose garden and at the back, seen through an archway, was the promise of an even more spacious garden, richly lawned.

'What a gorgeous place! Whose is it?'

'Yours—and mine.'

'Ours!' Lily was too stunned to notice the definite break between Ronan's words. 'But how?'

'I bought it. Isn't that how one usually acquires a house?'

'Of course I know that!' Lily aimed a playful punch at his arm. 'When did you...?'

'I signed the contracts last week. Oh, I know...' He'd seen her expression and interpreted it with almost telepathic accuracy. 'Connor said I should have consulted with you, but as soon as I saw the place I knew that you'd love it.'

'And you were right.'

Lily let the fact that he had understood her so well ease the sharp sting that had come with the thought that he had autocratically taken charge of everything without a word to her. What she found harder to accept was the fact that his best friend had known about the house—her marital home—before she had.

'Well, the two of us would have been far too cramped in that little flat of yours. This place is near enough to town for you to travel in every day and keep an eye on your business. After all, as the owner of Edgerton's most up and coming floral design business you should live somewhere rather more elegant than a one-bedroomed box.'

'And it's not too far from the motorway, so you can get to and from London.'

'Mmm—seen enough? Because from the look of the clouds gathering there's a storm about to break directly overhead. If we don't get inside soon we'll be soaked before we even reach the door.'

Ronan was quickly proved right. They had barely unloaded the cases from the car and deposited them in the black and white tiled hall when the first crash of thunder sounded, followed seconds later by the lash of rain against the windows.

'Oh, that was close!' Lily jumped exaggeratedly, huddling close to Ronan.

'You're not scared of thunder?'

'Not me.' She lifted laughing eyes to his disbelieving face. 'But it was a good excuse to get myself into your arms so that I could do this...'

Drawing his dark head down, she kissed him long and hard, tantalising his lips open with small, seductive darts of her tongue. Her private hope was that this was all the encouragement he would need to take things further, but, although his response was satisfactorily passionate, he made no attempt to deepen the caress, instead easing himself from her grasp and capturing her wandering hands in one of his.

'Enough of that! Don't you want to see your new home?'

'The bedrooms, perhaps.' Lily's smile was roguish. 'The rest of the house will still be there afterwards... No?' She could not believe it when he shook his head.

After weeks of abstinence throughout their admittedly brief courtship, she had been so sure that Ronan would be impatient to consummate their marriage. In her own mind, she had been absolutely convinced that they would barely get inside their room before he would make passionate love to her. But that had been when she had believed that he was taking her to a hotel room, not this lovely house.

'Later.' His smile grew when he saw her mutinous face. 'Lily, I want this to be just right. I want everything to go exactly as I planned, so please, bear with me.'

A flash of lightning seared across the sky, illuminating the strong-boned features of his face and making his eyes gleam like silver.

'Believe me, it will be worth waiting for.'

The words, the deep, intent voice in which they were spoken, and the burningly sensual look that accompanied them, all combined to send a shiver of delighted anticipation down Lily's spine as her momentary disappointment fled to be replaced by a tingle of excitement.

He was right. Delaying now would only add to the pleasure of what was to come. They should pace themselves slowly, savour the anticipation, let their appetites grow until they could hold back no longer. They had all the time in the world; there was no need to pounce on each other like gluttons at a feast table, cramming tasty morsels into their mouths with indiscriminate greed.

'I'll hold you to that promise,' she told him huskily. 'But, until that time comes, I suppose I'll have to settle for the guided tour.'

It was a large house, full of intriguing little corridors and unexpected corners, and by the time they had inspected every nook and cranny it was completely dark. The thunder had receded to a low grumble in the distance and the lightning no longer blazed across the sky. The ending of the storm had left quite a chill in the air, and when they returned to the elegant sitting room Lily couldn't suppress a faint shiver at the noticeable drop in temperature.

'You're cold.' Ronan frowned his concern. 'Shall I light a fire before we have supper?'

Lily's eyes followed the direction of his gesture towards the large open fireplace, topped by a wooden mantelpiece and framed by Victorian flowered tiles, and the shiver became more exaggerated, turning into a shudder of genuine fear.

'No! Thanks,' she added hastily.

'But it is a lot cooler in here, and it would be romantic to sit by the light of the flames.'

The light of the flames...

In her mind Lily unwillingly found herself dragged back into the past. She could see another room, one so very different from the spacious green and gold one in which she stood. She could see the cosy, slightly shabby décor and furniture, the Christmas tree standing in one corner, the paper chains on the walls. And on the mantelpiece cotton wool had been arranged to look like a snow scene, with miniature houses, fir trees, Santa Claus and a tiny sleigh pulled by model reindeer.

Below, in the grate, the crackle of the log fire. Before its flames stood a small, fair-haired figure, his hand outstretched towards a candle, freezing at her cry of warning. She had managed to stop Davey that time. But later... Later there had been the sudden flare of flames licking at the cotton wool, catching on the chains, leaping to the curtains, and suddenly all was fire, all alight, all...

'Lily?'

Jolted back to the present, she could only blink in confusion for a moment, until she realised who it was who stood before her, that it was Ronan who had spoken her name. And then it was an effort to force a smile.

'No fire, thanks. It's not *that* cold. All I need is a hot drink to warm me up—that and someone's arms around me.'

Some day she must tell Ronan the full story of that terrible night. She hadn't been able to bring herself to tell him exactly how her parents had died.

But not tonight. It wasn't the time or the place. It would spoil the atmosphere, ruin this special evening she had waited for— for an age, it seemed.

'Is there any food in this palace of yours?'

'But of course. I told you everything would be perfect. Come with me.'

He led her across the hall and into the large farmhouse kitchen, which was the only room in the house they hadn't yet visited. There, under covers on the scrubbed pine table, was a wonderful selection of all her favourite foods, carefully prepared and beautifully served on the finest china.

'Help yourself.'

To Lily's surprise she found that she was genuinely hungry. That morning she had been too on edge to eat anything substantial, and at the reception a blend of happiness and excitement had destroyed her appetite, so that now she was definitely ravenous. Picking up a plate, she selected several savoury treats and nibbled at them eagerly, nodding her thanks when Ronan set a glass of perfectly chilled wine on the table beside her.

'This is wonderful!' she exclaimed when her mouth was no longer full. 'Everything tastes so good.'

Suddenly supremely conscious of the way he had seated himself opposite her and was watching closely, not eating anything himself, she looked across at him questioningly, meeting those intent grey eyes that now seemed so dark, their irises almost twice their normal size.

'Aren't you hungry? This Brie is quite perfect. Try some...'

Breaking off a small piece, she held it out. But, instead of taking the fork from her, Ronan leaned forward until his face

was only inches away from hers, opening his mouth for the mor-
sel as a hungry child might.

With a smile, Lily placed the creamy cheese on his tongue,
then found herself transfixed, unable to look away, as he chewed,
then swallowed carefully. His eyes didn't leave hers as he let his
tongue slide out and slowly lick the taste from his lips.

'What else would you recommend?' he asked, his voice newly
husky, an octave deeper than before.

'The bread...'

A small, crusty piece, liberally spread with butter, followed
the cheese, but this time Lily used her fingers to feed him. Her
heart kicked against her ribs as she felt the warmth of his mouth
close about their tips.

'Some smoked salmon...and asparagus...and...'

She chose the items faster now, not wanting to look away from
him, her eyes returning swiftly to that darkly intent gaze while
her fingers moved blindly over the selection of dishes.

Her breathing was becoming less controlled, heated and uneven, in time with the thundering beat of her heart. Her body
felt as if it was bathed in the warm glow of bright sunlight instead
of the cool light of the moon. And the tiny hairs on the back of
her neck had lifted in instinctive awareness, bringing each nerve
shiveringly awake.

'Oh, and *strawberries*...'

This time he moved more swiftly than she had anticipated, and
she felt the graze of his teeth on her fingertips. The sensation
sent electrical pulses of reaction down her arm, making her
shiver in a very different response from the one she had felt
earlier. Her own mouth was dry, and she had to swallow sharply
to relieve the constriction there. Her lips, too, were uncomfortable, and her tongue snaked out to moisten them gently, her heart
turning over as she saw his cloudy gaze drop to follow the small,
sensual movement before flicking back to her now flushed face.

'Would you like some cream with that?'

Slowly she scooped some from the bowl, holding her finger
just inches from his mouth, knowing what would happen.

Ronan smiled slowly, seductively. Then with deliberate care
he leaned forward once more and took her into his warm, moist

mouth, licking the rich cream from her skin before he sucked gently along her finger's length. There could be no mistaking his meaning as he slid his lips up and down in a blatant likeness of another, far more intimate caress.

'*Ronan!*'

Unable to bear the tension any longer, she leaned across the table, easing her finger from his mouth and replacing it with her lips. The already frantic pounding of her heart threatened her ability to retain any degree of control as she savoured the erotic mixture of the taste of the cream, herself, and the intense, totally personal flavour of Ronan on her tongue.

When at last they had to break apart in order to breathe, Ronan drew back slowly and reluctantly, dragging in a raw-edged breath, his darkened eyes locked with hers.

'I think...' he said, slowly and hoarsely, his chest heaving as if he had just run a marathon. 'I think, my lady wife, that now is the time.'

And, getting to his feet, he held out his hand to her, strong, hard fingers locking with her paler, slender ones.

'Come with me,' he said, and it was part command, part awe-filled request. 'Come to bed. I want you now.'

The journey up to the bedroom took far longer than Lily could ever have anticipated. On each step Ronan paused to kiss her, every touch of his lips growing deeper, more passionate as they moved higher. And with each kiss her breathing grew faster, shallower, setting her head spinning, so that she couldn't think, couldn't form a single coherent word inside her thoughts.

She could only feel. Feel the pulsing excitement that flooded every inch of her body. Feel the growing need uncoiling, growing, spiralling deep inside her. Feel the heat of her blood, the thud of her heart, the ache of need that made her breasts swell and the most intimate point between her thighs throb with yearning sensation.

It seemed for ever until they reached the room. A lifetime before Ronan kicked the door closed and gathered her up into his arms. Sweeping one hand through the silken fall of her hair, he held her head immobile with one strong hand at the nape of her neck, bringing his dark head down sharply, crushing her lips under his in one final, wordless declaration of the passion he could now hold back no longer.

Lily could only respond in kind. Straining her body against his in a relentless need to get closer, to feel as much as was possible of his hard strength against hers, she abandoned all control. At last she could release all the pent-up frustrations of the past weeks, open herself to the deep-felt need to know everything there was to know about this man, experience the full, elemental force of his lovemaking. Her mouth kissed, clung, urged, demanded, inciting him to an electric build-up of passion, opening the floodgates of need, fully content in the knowledge that she would never be able to close them again.

When the erotic contact of their mouths became inadequate, they broke apart, each breathing heavily, eyeing each other with a wild excitement.

'Do I undress myself?' Lily asked unevenly. 'Or do you want to do it.'

'Oh, I want to,' Ronan assured her deeply. 'I want to more than all the world. But I warn you...'

One hand came out, slid a tiny button on the front of her bronze silk blouse with a delicate slowness that had her wriggling in impatient delight.

'I intend to enjoy every minute of it, every sight, every sound...' The corners of his mouth quirked up in delight when an uncontrollable whimper of response escaped her as a second button slipped from its mooring.

'Every scent...'

Lowering his proud head to the creamy curves his actions had exposed in the open neckline, he inhaled deeply, taking in the floral aroma of her perfume and the subtler, deeply personal fragrance of her skin.

'And every taste.'

Hot and wet, his tongue snaked out, tracing heated, erotic patterns across her skin, dipping down into the scented valley between her breasts. As Lily moaned her response she felt him smile against her flesh, the tiny movement making her nipples swell in yearning response, their hardened peaks straining against the lacy confines of the cobweb-fine bra she wore. Ronan's triumphant laughter shivered across her burning nerve-endings.

'More?'

'More!' It was a choking cry of heartfelt longing.

'More,' Ronan echoed, taking that tormenting mouth down and across the slope of one breast, sliding the softness of his lips along its satin curve until they closed over the aching nipple, suckling strongly.

With a gasp of delight, Lily's hands clenched in the auburn sleekness of his hair, holding him closer still, unable to get enough of this sweetly agonising pleasure. Her breath caught in her throat as she felt his teeth graze the sensitised bud, heightening her arousal even more with wicked expertise.

But a second later even that was not enough. While his attention was concentrated on one part of her there were other, equally sensitive areas that grew impatient, demanding the same voluptuous rapture.

And she was no longer content to be still. She wanted to feel him too, to touch his skin, explore every inch of his body, know him fully at last.

The silk jacket was clumsily tugged off and discarded carelessly on the floor, followed swiftly by his shirt and tie. The feel of the warm satin of his flesh under her fingertips acted like the flick of a switch, triggering off a wild yearning that had her flinging caution to the winds. Fingers trembling with need, she fumbled with the narrow leather belt around his waist, sighing her satisfaction as she pulled it free.

'Steady!' Ronan's voice was thick and hoarse, sounding a note of warning against her throat.

'Steady?' Lily muttered in impatient response. 'I want this— I want you!'

She was struggling to breathe, finding it almost impossible to drag enough air into her straining lungs. Every inch of her skin was burning up with hunger, heating her blood until it seemed to pool in a molten rush of heat and awareness between her thighs.

'Well, if that's what you want.' It was a low, contented growl. 'That's what you shall have.'

She was lifted from her feet and carried towards the bed. He lowered her on to the covers and his mouth locked with hers again, the sensual intrusion of his tongue tangling with her own until she moved against him restlessly. Sliding down beside her, he moved fluidly against her, the pressure of his lean body making her crave more intimate contact with a desperation that was like a scream through every nerve-end.

Her clothes, too, had been discarded somewhere, she had no idea when he had actually eased them from her body. But now he leaned above her, propped up on one arm, looking down at her with passion-darkened eyes.

'Tonight, my lady, you can have whatever you want.'

Later, that subtly emphasised *tonight* was to come back to haunt her bitterly. But for that night she had no sense of premonition, no hint of anything beyond her own pleasure.

'Whatever...' It was a sigh of sheer delight in the anticipation of what was to come.

'But first...'

Turning away from her for a moment, he reached for the small foil-wrapped package he had tossed on to the bedside cabinet and ripped it open.

'We don't need...' Lily began, but he silenced her with a gentle finger laid across her lips.

'Oh, yes, we do,' he insisted softly. 'A child doesn't come into my plans at all right now. I want you all to myself for a long time, without any such complication.'

All to myself. The whispered words sent of glow of sheer joy through every inch of Lily's body, making her purr like a contented cat.

'That's fine by me.'

Lazily she let her fingers drift over the powerful muscles of his back and shoulders, sliding into the dark silk of his hair. Feeling its unexpected lack of length, the bluntness of the line at the base of his finely shaped skull, she frowned in sensual disapproval.

'Why did you cut your hair?' she complained softly.

'Perhaps I thought it didn't suit my new status as a married man.'

'But if you knew how long I've dreamed of this moment, how I wanted to run my fingers through it...'

She suited action to the words.

'Trace its path right down to your shoulders...'

The way his long body tensed, then jerked convulsively under her caress told her of the effect she was having, bringing a smile of dreamy triumph to her lips.

'Along your back...'

Her forefinger trailed all the way down the strong, straight line of his spine and under the loosened trousers, moving teasingly over the tautly muscled buttocks.

'Witch!' Ronan growled. 'You're asking for trouble.'

'Really?'

Lily rounded her eyes with mock surprise and shock.

'Do you know?' she murmured. 'I think that's exactly what I'm doing.'

Her wandering fingers moved to close over the waistband of his trousers. With Ronan's willing help he was soon free of his only remaining clothing, a faintly shaken laugh escaping him as she explored his naked body without restraint.

Her hunger doubling with every second, she moved sinuously against his naked form, revelling in the abrasion of the curls of his body hair against her breasts, the warmth of his flat stomach next to hers. Lower still, the hard, heated force of his physical arousal lay like burning velvet against her thighs, making her yearn and ache with a hunger that could no longer be denied.

'Ronan, please...' she heard herself beg.

But Ronan had yet more skills in his repertoire, and he used them with the consummate artistry of genius, touching, stroking, kissing, taking tiny, sharp little bites at her skin. And when his knowing fingers found the warm, moist innermost core of her femininity she gasped out loud, twisting in total loss of control.

Frantic heat pulsed through her, radiating out from that aching spot deep at the heart of her being, and she knew nothing beyond that tiny focus, her whole thought process suspended in concentration on it. Each time she thought she could bear no more he found another variation on delight, another refinement of pleasure, and the intensity of her need increased until it was nearer to torture than rapture.

Only then did he slide over her, nudging her thighs apart with the hair-roughened strength of his. For a split second he hesitated, and she saw something flare in his darkened eyes that made her heart jolt in instinctive panic. But a second later the moment was forgotten as he entered her with a single fierce thrust, driving any chance of thought away for ever.

Lily lost her sense of time, of space, of being. She lost herself and became only one part of the whole they made together. Her hands clenched over the powerful muscles of his shoulders, her spine arching in desperate need to feel to the uttermost every urgent touch, every move of his body on hers. She was soaring higher and higher, spiralling wildly towards a blazing sun that would burn her up, leave her as nothing but ashes, and she didn't care. All that mattered was reaching that peak of fulfilment.

As the final burning wave broke over her she heard a voice, ragged and hoarse, crying Ronan's name out loud, and realised with a sense of shock that it was her own. The sound was so wild, so primitive she couldn't recognise herself in it. Adrift on a heated sea of delight, she heard Ronan, too, cry out as he followed her into the oblivion of ecstasy.

But it wasn't her name that was torn from his lips at the height of his passion. Nor was it any soft word of love nor expression of the pleasure that had possessed him. Instead it was a wild and husky sound that seemed to have been dragged from the depths of his soul.

'Remember!' he said. 'Remember this, my Lily! Remember!'

Remember. Lily could only think hazily when the final storm had faded, ebbing slowly away like warm, sluggish waves lapping a sun-heated shore. *Remember.* How could she ever forget? How could there be any doubt that she would recall this first night of her marriage in every tiny detail?

Each moment of it was etched on to her brain, second by second, and while she lived nothing would ever erase them from her memory. Of course she would always remember. The whole experience had been totally unforgettable.

CHAPTER THREE

UNFORGETTABLE.

The word seared inside Lily's head, making her feel chilled to the bone. If the nightmare into which she had woken was all that remained of her married life, how could she ever survive with those scenes of overwhelming passion engraved on her soul?

But she had to come out of her memories because Ronan had said something she hadn't heard, let alone understood, and she could only blink at him in blank incomprehension.

'I think we'd better talk indoors.'

Talk? Lily eyed him with wary suspicion.

'Talk' sounded hopeful. It made it seem as if there was some room for discussion, not just the unequivocal ultimatum he had handed out at the start.

But 'indoors' meant going into the house, and that meant getting down from her position on the car. That might be decidedly incongruous, possibly even close to looking ridiculous, but if it stopped him driving off, as he had obviously intended, then it was her only small advantage, and right now she intended to hang on to it.

'Is there anything to talk about?' she questioned edgily. 'I mean, you present me with a *fait accompli* and then you say we can negotiate...'

She broke off sharply as she saw his dark head move in fierce negation, the coppery strands catching the sun with a disturbingly attractive effect.

'No negotiation,' he declared adamantly. 'I just want you to listen...'

'Then I'm not moving! You can talk to me right here.'

She tried to sit up straighter, needing to outface him. But the unwary movement on the polished metal proved her undoing. The silky robe gave her no grip, so that she had to put her hands down flat in order to stop herself from sliding ignominiously off on to the ground.

'Oh, for God's sake!'

Ronan's fury was expressed in a darkly eloquent stream of violent curses as he strode forward sharply.

Lily had no time to guess at his plan, or to prepare herself in any way. An awkward, fearful squawk of protest escaped her as one arm closed around her shoulders, the other slid under her thighs, and she was lifted bodily from the car.

'Ronan! Put me down!'

Her wild objection went unheeded. He simply tightened his grip, clamping his arms around her with the bruising effect of steel bands until she was incapable of movement, as he marched towards the house.

'I never did carry you over the threshold,' he muttered, the sardonic humour scraping her nerves raw as she, too, recognised in his actions the black parody of the old-fashioned tradition of the groom carrying his bride into their first marital home. Ronan kicked open the nearest door, striding into the elegant green and gold living room and dumping her unceremoniously into an armchair.

'Now—oh, no you don't!'

He reacted swiftly when she would have got to her feet in an attempt at escape. One strong hand fastened punishingly on her shoulder again, pushing her back into the chair and holding her there.

'What sort of joke is this, Ronan? It's not funny, believe me. I—'

'No joke,' he insisted harshly. 'Do I look like I'm laughing?'

If the truth be told, Ronan reflected inwardly, humour had never been further from his mind. He just wanted this whole thing over and done with.

He had never expected her to fight so hard, or for so long. He had thought that by now he would be well away from Edgerton, his mission accomplished, leaving the shattered pieces of his so-called marriage well behind for Davey Cornwell to pick up, if he ever resurfaced.

Instead, he was still here, unable to get away. Lily seemed to have entwined herself around his life like a clinging vine, and, what was worse, he actually found himself starting to feel sorry for her. He had to get a grip on himself. Pity was an emotion he couldn't afford to let himself experience.

'Answer me one thing.' The conflict he was enduring inside made his voice even harsher than he had intended. 'Were you telling the truth when you said you liked this house?'

The abrupt change of tack totally nonplussed Lily. Even though she could see no reason for the question she could only answer it straight.

'Of course. I love it; it's quite beautiful. But...'

Ronan dismissed her confused question with an imperious wave of his free hand.

'Then it's yours.'

Hearing that, Lily felt that if she hadn't been sitting down already she might actually have fallen. The ground seemed to have crumbled away beneath her feet, leaving her with nothing firm enough on which to stand.

'But it must be worth a fortune!'

'Something like that,' Ronan agreed with supreme indifference. 'But I knew that if I actually went ahead and married you there would be legal repercussions. I accept that I shall have to support—'

'I don't want your money! You know that's not why I married you!'

'Well, it's all that's on offer. There's nothing else.'

'But why?'

If his behaviour had been incomprehensible before, now it was totally beyond belief, making her shake her head in bewilderment.

'Why did you marry me if...?'

She couldn't continue, transfixed by a sudden wild, savage look in those translucent eyes. But the dangerous light that froze her tongue was belied by the indolent way he lifted his broad shoulders in a dismissive shrug.

'Don't ask, Lily,' he warned. 'You wouldn't like the answer.'

Whatever bitter satisfaction he might derive from telling her the whole story, he had promised himself that that would be

Cornwell's job. Let Davey explain things, if he dared. Let him face up to just what it meant to have his sister's life ruined, her future lying in tatters, because of his own wicked behaviour.

'It's not the answer that worries me!' Lily retorted. 'It's the question and the fact that you've forced me to ask it.'

Dear God, please let him not see how much that last comment had affected her! Her stomach churned sickeningly, her head spinning dreadfully.

It was the casual lack of emotion that hurt more than anything. The way that he had kept the level of his voice relaxed, conversational, while hers came and went like a badly tuned radio.

Was this really the man she had promised to love and honour for the rest of her life? The man who had vowed the same to *her* only the day before.

Behind her a clock struck ten-thirty, and a cold, sharp knife stabbed at her with the memory of the way that at just this time twenty-four hours ago she had been coming back from the hairdresser's with Hannah, laughing and excited, her heart light with anticipation of the happiness ahead of her.

But she had felt nervous too, the full importance of what she was about to do always at the forefront of her mind. She hadn't gone into her marriage lightly, while Ronan...

'"Don't ask" just isn't good enough!'

Anger giving her a strength she hadn't known she possessed, she pushed his hand away and got to her feet in a rush, flames blazing in the golden depths of her eyes.

'You made certain vows yesterday, and so did I. I *meant* those vows, Ronan! Every single word of them! I wanted to love you and live with you, have your children...'

Had she finally got through to him? Certainly there seemed to be a change in his set expression, his head going back sharply, heavy lids hooding those steely eyes.

'And I thought you meant them too! If you didn't—if you got me here under false pretences—then the least you can do is give me some sort of an explanation. You owe me that if nothing else.'

'I *owe*...!'

The dangerous undertone was positively terrifying, but Lily

couldn't afford to let herself be affected by it. She felt as if she was fighting for her life, which, in a way, she was. She was fighting for the life she had believed she was going to have, her future as a married woman—as Ronan's wife.

'I want an answer, Ronan!'

This time his gaze actually dropped from her face, as if he could no longer bear her furiously injured glare. Those slate coloured eyes lowered, slanted downwards, and then suddenly held, as if transfixed.

'Ronan!'

'Cover yourself up.' It sounded thick and raw.

'What?'

'I said *cover yourself up*!'

It was only when his hands came out, closing on the front of the mint-green robe and yanking the two sides of it together, that she realised how her unthinking movement in leaping to her feet had wrenched at the already insecurely fastened garment, pulling it apart. Her neck and shoulders, the soft curves of her breasts were exposed to his darkened gaze, the creamy skin flushed, like her face, with a mixture of confusion and tension.

'You may have distracted me that way last night,' Ronan grated. 'But not this time.'

'And I may have let you paw me then,' Lily flung back, pulling away from him as violently as she could while still preserving some small degree of modesty. 'But never again!'

The memory of the feel of those beautifully shaped hands on her skin, on all the intimate pleasure spots on her body made her feel nauseous, and she struggled to erase all the hurt and distress from her voice, thankful to hear it sound as cold and brittle as she could wish.

'Last night you didn't call it *pawing*,' Ronan told her with a cruel smile. 'Last night you wanted all I could give you. You begged...'

'Last night I believed that we were *married*!'

'So you did.' Ronan nodded coldly. 'And that's the real bottom line in all this, isn't it, my darling?'

His tone took the words to a point a million miles away from an endearment.

'So, do you really want to know why I married you?'

No! Lily's heart pleaded with her to say it. To declare that, no, she didn't want to know anything about it. Didn't want to hear a word he had to say.

If she had had any hope of salvation earlier, when she had run after him, it had died a slow and painful death. If any such illusion had bolstered her up, giving her the determination to jump up on the bonnet of the Mercedes, then there was none left now. It had all evaporated like mist before the sun, leaving her weak and defenceless, vulnerable to anything he might choose to throw at her.

But rationally she had to know. She couldn't accept it as the truth unless she heard it from his own mouth. And so, in spite of herself, and against the pleading protests of her wounded heart, she found herself nodding, forming a whispered, 'Yes,' with parched lips.

There was no way he could tell her the truth. Not when she looked at him with those big golden eyes, seeming for all the world like a wounded fawn trapped by the hounds and totally at the end of its tether. Silently he cursed her missing brother, wishing with all his heart that he could get his hands around Davey Cornwell's throat and press hard.

But he had to say something. Something monstrous enough to make her let him go and stop her coming after him—for her own sake as much as for his own.

'It was the only way you would let me near you,' he said, so carelessly that for the space of a couple of heartbeats Lily didn't quite register exactly what he meant. 'And I wanted you so much that I was quite prepared...'

He never completed the sentence. Without even forming a rational thought, Lily lifted her hand and lashed out violently. The crack of her palm making painful contact with his cheek sounded disturbingly loud and brutal, its echoes seeming to linger in the sudden silence that followed.

Ronan swallowed hard, just once, then directed that fiendish smile straight into her blazing eyes.

'I told you you wouldn't like the answer.'

'You bastard!' It was low, fiercely controlled, filled with all the malevolence she could summon up.

Just for a second a flare of something dangerous in his eyes made her fearful of retribution, but then abruptly he seemed to recollect himself, and shook his head slightly.

'I think I deserved that,' he said, with a shocking calmness that rocked her sense of reality. 'Do you feel better now?'

'I could hardly feel any worse!'

At this moment she couldn't even see why she had ever loved him, or convinced herself that she did. Because surely she must have been bitterly mistaken, totally self-deceiving. Surely she could never have cared for a man like this.

But the Ronan she had met and fallen in love with hadn't been like this.

No!

Ruthlessly she crushed down the weak thought, refusing to let it take root in her mind. The Ronan she had believed herself in love with and the fiend who now stood before her were one and the same man. To think anything else was to weaken herself, to give him a chance to hurt her all over again.

'Get out, Ronan,' she said, and was glad to hear that her voice was as coolly controlled as his own. He could be in no doubt as to the strength of her conviction.

And to judge by his expression he knew only too well that she meant what she said.

'Get out and don't come back.'

'If you remember, that was what I had planned in the first place. You were the one who dragged me back.'

'Well, I'd rather die than do any such thing now. All I want is to see the back of you, once and for all.'

'Which suits me fine. Goodbye, Lily, I wish I could say it's been fun.'

He sketched a small, mocking bow before turning on his heel.

Mutely Lily watched him go, past knowing what she felt, torn between relief and bitter despair. He was almost at the door when he paused and slowly turned back.

'You were right, of course, darling. I am a bastard. But perhaps you should ask yourself how I came to be that way.'

'I don't care! I don't want to know—I don't want to know *anything* about you! For one thing, how would I be able to tell what was the truth and what was lies?'

'The truth.' It was a harshly cynical laugh, totally devoid of humour. 'Oh, yes, the truth. Well, Lily my love, if you want the whole truth it's not me you should come to. You see, that question you were so upset about is only one small part of things. If you want to know the whole story then you really should ask your brother—if he'll tell you. Now this time I really am going.'

And this time she let him go. She had to. There was nothing else that she could do.

As she stood and watched him walk away, saw him climb into his car and start the engine with a roar that spoke of a mood far removed from his usual calm control, the clock in the hallway struck the hour again.

Lily dug her teeth down hard into her bottom lip, refusing to let the tears fall until Ronan was out of sight.

It was twelve o'clock. At this time yesterday she had stood on the steps of the church, smiling and happy, her brand-new husband at her side. She had been his wife for just twenty-four hours and now it was all over.

High above her head, the sun was shining in the clear blue sky. It was a perfect spring day. A perfect day on which to start what should have been a perfect married life. Instead it was the day that marked the end of her marriage before it had even begun.

CHAPTER FOUR

'ASK your brother...ask your brother...'

Ronan's parting shot became a nagging refrain in Lily's thoughts over the next four days.

'That question...is only one small part of things. If you want to know the whole story then you really should ask your brother—if he'll tell you.'

She would if she could. But she had no idea where Davey was, or even if he was still in the country.

When she and Ronan had set the date for their ill-fated wedding, she had done everything she could to track down her missing brother, but with no success. All leads had turned into dead-ends, and his former friends were as much in the dark as to his whereabouts as she was. It was as if Davey had vanished off the face of the earth.

The absence of her brother from her life had been a source of distress to Lily for over three years now. Ever since the day of his seventeenth birthday, when she had returned home to find his room uncharacteristically neat and tidy, his wardrobe empty of the jeans and tee shirts that were the only clothes he wore. But it had been when she had discovered that his guitar had gone that she knew things were serious.

Davey's beloved Gibson Les Paul, paid for with the earnings from many hours of paper rounds, Saturday jobs and, in the last year, lessons that he had given to other young aspiring musicians, was like a part of him. If he had it with him, then it meant he wasn't coming back in the near future.

And if she had had any doubts or hopes left, then the note she found on her own pillow had dispelled them all: "Gone to make my name and fortune. Look out for me on the telly very soon!"

And he had signed it, as he now signed everything, scorning the family name he thought too childish for a would-be rock star, with the single initial 'D'.

Second only to her parents' untimely deaths, Davey's desertion had hit her hard. With time, the pain of his abrupt departure had only faded into an aching sense of loss, not vanished altogether, and she lived with the feeling of there being a gap in her life that no one else could fill.

And Ronan had known that. Known it and yet kept his thoughts on the matter to himself.

Because now, with one of those bitter ironies that haunted her thoughts by day and kept her from sleep by night, it seemed that *Ronan* was the one person who had had any contact with her brother in the time since he had left home.

'If you want to know the whole story then you really should ask your brother...'

It could mean only one thing. Davey, wild, foolish Davey, had done something to bring down Ronan's fury on his head, spark off this burning need to hurt and destroy. But what could be so bad that it had resulted in such a terrible revenge?

Just what had Davey done?

She would have to start her investigations all over again. Go back and check every lead, every contact, however vague. Once more she would have to try and find her errant brother, but this time her search would be so much more important. It would be given that added edge by the devouring need to find out just how he had become involved with Ronan and what had happened as a result.

But first there was something else she had to do, something she dreaded but knew she couldn't avoid. She couldn't hide away here in this house for the rest of her life. Sooner or later the news would leak out that her marriage had failed before it had even begun, and she could just imagine what sort of stories would be concocted to explain her personal tragedy.

The longer she waited before showing her face, the worse it would become, and she had always believed that if she had something unpleasant to do it was best to get it over and done with.

She gave herself the week of what should have been her honeymoon to hide away in the lovely house. To lick her wounds and weep the tears she vowed she would never show in public. And when that week was up she gathered together the shattered remnants of her self-control, cobbling them together into the closest she could come to a sort of armour to put around herself, and prepared to face the world again.

But she wouldn't have been human if she hadn't felt the need for some support, a back-up team to help her over the worst. And so, acting quickly before her nerve failed her completely, she dialled her best friend's number first.

'Hannah? It's Lily. I'm afraid I've got some really bad news...'

She could only hope that the story would be a nine-day wonder.

That hope was not to be fulfilled. Four weeks after her return to work, the small town was still buzzing with the story of the marriage that had never been.

'It's not fair!' Lily complained to Hannah, when her friend called at the shop on her way home from the school where she taught History. 'You'd think something else would have happened by now to take the heat off me.'

'But that's just the point,' her friend commiserated dryly. 'Nothing does happen here, so your misfortune was God's gift to the local gossips. And really you can hardly blame them. After all, Edgerton had never seen such excitement as there was over your wedding. You've got to admit that Ronan isn't exactly typical of the sort of man we see around here.'

'You can say that again.' Lily sighed despondently, recalling the way she had felt when she had first set eyes on his tall, lean frame, the stunning bone structure of his face, the striking steel blue of his eyes under the burnished colour of his hair.

'And as something of a local entrepreneur yourself...'

'Entrepreneur! Oh, come on!' Lily scoffed, rather more emphatically than she'd actually meant because she was trying to distract her thoughts from the painful path they were following.

She didn't want to think about Ronan. Didn't want to recall how he had affected her right from the start, the forceful impact of his potent masculinity going straight to her heart like an arrow speeding to the gold on a target.

'And how many other local women do you know who have set themselves up in business on one small market stall and within six years earned a reputation as the best flower arranger—sorry, floral designer—in the county?' Hannah enquired reprovingly.

That was how she'd first met Ronan, Lily recalled miserably. She had been asked to do the flowers at the wedding of the only daughter of a wealthy local industrialist. As a business associate of Frank Hodgson, Ronan had been amongst the guests. They had been introduced by the bride's mother, he had asked her to dance, and the rest, with a sort of inevitability, had been history.

'I've been lucky.'

'Lucky!' her friend snorted. 'Lily, luck had nothing to do with it. Talent and sheer determined hard work is more like it. You pulled yourself up again after a loss that would have floored most people—particularly considering you weren't even out of your teens when it happened—and you've gone on to make a real success of your life. *And* you brought up Davey too, while you did so. If anyone deserves some happiness now, it's you. I thought you had found it with Ronan.'

Hannah's face changed, her normally smiling expression becoming hard and hostile.

'If I could get my hands on him...'

'Hannah, please!' Lily put in hastily.

They had been over and over the story of Ronan's desertion until she was sick to death of it, and they were no nearer an answer than they had ever been.

At least in the past few weeks she had learned if not to adjust then to find a way of living with what had happened. The wounds Ronan had inflicted on her were too deep, too agonising to be anywhere close to healing, but by throwing herself into her work she had found a way of distracting herself from the pain.

'I don't want to talk about it. I don't even want to *think*...'

Luckily, at that moment they were interrupted by the sound of a knock, and Heather, her junior assistant, put her head round the door.

'A visitor for you, Lily. Personal, he said.'

'Personal, *he* said.' Lily's heart leapt so painfully that her breath tangled in her throat. *Could* it be? Was it possible?

She didn't know whether she was hopeful or fearful, how she

would feel or what she could say if it did turn out to be Ronan. But she was still struggling for some degree of composure when her already shaky mental state was knocked even further off balance as her visitor appeared in the doorway.

Not Ronan. This man had hair as fair as her own, but with a silvery cast where hers was pure gold, falling to his shoulders in a long, straggly tangle. Eyes a darker brown than her amber, looking even more so in contrast to the unhealthy pallor of thin cheeks that were all planes and shadows. A tall, gangling frame just emerging into full manhood from adolescence, but so painfully thin that her heart clenched in distress at the sight.

'*Davey!*'

He was the last person she had expected to see, and all the pain of the missing three years sounded in her voice.

Davey caught it, and his mouth twisted as he shuffled awkwardly from one foot to another.

'Hi, Sis! Surprised to see me?' It was faintly cocky, more than half defiant, as if he was unsure of his welcome.

'Surprised...' Lily's voice was choked and uneven. 'Oh, Davey!'

Released from the numbing sense of shock into which his appearance had thrown her, she got to her feet and rushed to his side, her arms going out to enclose him in a warm, welcoming hug. She couldn't help wincing in distress as she felt just how little flesh there was on his tall, delicate frame.

Whatever Davey had been doing, clearly he hadn't achieved the success he had dreamed of. It was obvious that he hadn't been eating properly for quite some time.

'It's been so long! Where've you been? I've missed you so much!'

'Missed you too.'

The reluctance with which Davey submitted to her hug made it plain that he was embarrassed by the display of emotion in front of Hannah. In deference to his feelings, Lily eased up, releasing him even though her own instinct was to hold him tight and never let him go. Hannah was not so sensitive to his feelings.

'It's about time you got in touch, young man. Your sister's been out of her mind with worry. Don't you think that it would have been thoughtful to let her know where you were once in a while?'

'I was—busy.' Davey rubbed the side of one scuffed leather boot against the other. 'Time just got away from me.'

'How much time does it take to make a phone call?'

'Hannah!' Lily put in hastily. 'He's here now. That's all that matters. Are you staying for a while, Davey?' She tried to make it sound as casual as possible.

'If that's OK.'

Suddenly he looked straight at her, bruised-looking lids narrowing over wide-pupilled brown eyes.

'I heard you were looking for me. Is there something wrong?'

'Wrong!' Even Lily's reproachful frown couldn't keep Hannah's mouth shut. 'That is a major understatement.'

For the first time a flash of concern showed on Davey's face as he turned to his sister.

'What...?'

'I wasn't looking for you because something was wrong, Davey,' Lily said quickly. He looked wary enough already, like a nervous horse on the point of bolting. She couldn't risk saying something that might drive him to do just that. 'I was—getting married, and I wanted you at the wedding.'

It hurt so much to say it. Each word was like another slash of a knife into an already lacerated heart.

'But in the end perhaps it's just as well you weren't there, because things didn't turn out the way I'd hoped.'

'The way you had a right to *expect*!' Hannah put in indignantly. 'If I could get my hands on Ronan Guerin...'

'*Ronan Guerin!*'

It was just as Lily had feared. Davey reacted as if he had just been subjected to the most appalling electric shock, his head going back, bruised eyes widening. Lily would have sworn that it was impossible for his skin to lose any more colour, but it had become positively ashen.

'You tangled with Ronan Guerin?'

'How do you know about him?'

Lily had to force the words from a painfully dry throat. Ronan's final declaration that she should ask her brother for the truth swirled inside her head, all the ominous undertones of menacing threat that had darkened it made so much worse by Davey's panicked reaction. And that 'tangled with' sounded disturbingly foreboding.

'Anyone who's lived in London for any time knows Guerin. He owns acres of property there, including some of the most glamorous addresses around. They call him the Resurrector, because he has this uncanny knack of finding an ailing business, buying it up cheap, then turning it around and making it a howling success. If he takes an interest in you, you're made—usually,' he amended, with a painful adjustment that tightened the knots in Lily's nerves to screaming pitch.

'What happened, Davey?' she forced herself to ask.

'Guerin's after me. I...'

Her brother looked across at Hannah, who, Lily was thankful to see, took the unsubtle hint immediately.

'It's time I was off. I'll see you, Lily.'

Lily barely noticed her leave, her attention focused on Davey's pale face. He had moved to perch on one side of the desk, one leg swinging nervously, and her fearful mood was in no way eased by the way his long, narrow hands were twisted together, clenched until the knuckles showed white.

'What happened?'

'I was working in a club as a barman...'

Davey's eyes wouldn't meet hers but were fixed on a spot on the carpet several feet in front of him.

'One night the regular entertainer didn't turn up, so I stood in for him. It just happened that that was a night when Ronan was in the place and he heard me sing. He talked to me afterwards, said how much he'd enjoyed my performance and asked if I'd ever thought of turning professional. When I said that was my dream, he told me he might be able to help, but first he wanted to make sure he wasn't wasting his time. I didn't really expect to hear any more about it, but the next night he turned up again, this time with a business associate—an independent record producer—who talked about offering me a recording contract.'

'But that's wonderful!'

The words shrivelled on Lily's tongue as Davey lifted his head and turned darkly sceptical eyes on her.

'Think so? That's what I believed too—at first. I was over the moon.'

He lifted his thin shoulders in a shrug that dismissed those thoughts as foolish and impossibly naïve.

'It didn't last.' The bleak despondency of his words was a deathblow to any hopes that Lily still had left.

'What went wrong?' Because obviously something had gone very badly wrong, or Davey would not be here now, in this state, and Ronan would not be somewhere hunting for him, like a hungry tiger deprived of his prey.

'I screwed up.' Davey ran a shaky hand through his lank hair and sighed deeply, his eyes sliding away from the concern in hers. 'Messed up big time. You don't want to know.'

'Davey, *tell me*!'

'Look, Lill, this wasn't my first chance at a recording career. When I first went to London I met up with a guy—I'll spare you the details, but the end result was that I was locked into this bitch of a contract. Basically, I did all the work and he got the profits. It didn't take me long to realise I'd been taken for a mug, but by then it was too late. They owned me—for the rest of my life, it seemed. I did the only thing I could think of—I ran, broke my contract, left the whole thing. I even changed my name. That's how I ended up in the barman job.'

His mouth twisted into a wry grin.

'So I couldn't take on any other contract, could I? But that was where Guerin really surprised me. He offered to buy me out of the bad contract—at a price.'

Hearing Lily's exclamation of shock, Davey nodded, his mouth twisting wryly.

'Yeah, it stunned me too. But this mate of his had made it clear that my career was a sound investment. And that was what Guerin was interested in—the money, not the music. I was another failing business he planned on resurrecting.'

A touch of the old Davey revived as he lifted his head and gave her a small, arrogant smile.

'He had it on strong authority that I was good, that given a chance I could earn him back every penny he'd invested—and more. But of course he wanted everything signed and legally watertight. And then— Oh, Sis, you can guess what it was like. I had a tiny taste of success—the applause, the audiences...'

'Surely I would have heard...'

'Oh, I was hardly Top Twenty material, not yet. I couldn't rush straight into the recording studio at first. I had to start to earn something of a reputation in the clubs down south. And I was doing that. But I—went off my head a little. More than a little. There were a couple of gigs I messed up, got too drunk to play properly. Another one I didn't turn up for. Guerin was furious. He'd spent a fortune on me—even bought me the guitar and amps I needed, and a van to transport them in—and I was losing him money. The last straw was when I crashed the van and all the gear went up in flames. I'd told him I'd get it insured, but I hadn't got round to actually doing anything about it.'

'Oh, Davey!'

'I know!' Her brother grimaced at the reproach in her voice, still refusing to meet her eyes. 'I know I was a complete idiot. I just lost my grip. But Guerin had me so tied up in all these legal tangles that I ended up in a worse position than ever. So I took the same route as before—I just split—got out. But legally I'm still tied to Guerin, so now *he's* after me for breach of contract. And he's charging interest on what he loaned me at an obscene rate. He knows there's no way I'll ever be able to pay, but he's still after my blood.'

Lily shivered at the thought of Ronan's cold, implacable fury. If she hadn't seen that, she might have thought that Davey was inclined to exaggerate, but the memory of the ruthless, unyielding way Ronan had ended their marriage left her in no doubt that he was telling nothing less than the truth.

'I was supposed to make him a fortune; instead I lost him one. I let him down and he's determined I should pay for that.'

'But surely if you talked to him—apologised, it could still be put right,' Lily put in earnestly. 'He believed you had talent once, he must still think it now. If you admitted you'd been a fool, said you'd work really hard and pay back everything you owe, however long it takes, wouldn't he listen?'

Davey's expressive shudder was answer enough, without a word having to be spoken, and his pale cheeks turned grey just at the thought of what she was suggesting.

'It's gone way past that, Lill. I could never replace what he's lost, and, to be frank, Guerin wants much more than repayment. I daren't face him, Sis. He's after revenge and nothing else will do.'

Revenge. The word brought a sour, foul taste into Lily's mouth, sickening her. Had Ronan's courtship of her been just part of a campaign of revenge against her brother? Had her fiasco of a wedding been just cold-blooded manipulation, the man she had loved simply using her feelings to further his own callous ends?

And had it all been about *money*? Was Ronan's motivation really so base, so mercenary that he had done all this, treated her so cruelly, taken her love and broken it into tiny pieces, destroyed her life, just because of a bad debt? Even when Davey put it into figures, quoting an amount that made her head spin, she still couldn't believe that Ronan had been prepared to stoop so low.

Belatedly Davey seemed to recall just why they had started on this conversation in the first place.

'But what is it with you and Ronan Guerin? Your friend said—'

'Oh, don't worry about Hannah,' said Lily hastily.

Davey had enough on his plate as it was, and besides, she had only just got him back after the long years of separation. If he learned the truth about her connection with Ronan he might just turn and run again, and this time she'd never find him. Time enough to let him know all the gory details when she had no alternative.

'There's no need to let that trouble you.'

Just to see the relief on his pale face, the way the gaunt body relaxed back against the desk made it worth the stress of hiding the facts from him.

'It's so good to see you, Lill,' he said jerkily. 'I didn't know where else to go. But I knew you'd be all right, that you'd look after me the way you always did. Lily—can I stay for a while?'

Lily's heart twisted in a bittersweet mixture of delight and nervous apprehension. For so long she had dreamed of Davey coming home, of him saying just that, and at times she had feared that he never would. Now at last he was here, with her, but the thought of Ronan and his malign influence over both her life and her brother's cast a dark shadow over her happiness.

'*Please*, Sis!'

The uncertainty in her brother's plea made her realise that she was frowning, that he had interpreted the expression her thoughts had put on to her face as reluctance to have him back in her life. That was the last thing she wanted him to feel she reproved herself, forcing a smile.

'Of course you can stay, kid. For as long as you like.'

With a struggle she pushed all thoughts of Ronan to the back of her mind, refusing to let them spoil her delight in seeing Davey again.

'I'll get my coat and we'll go now. I'll knock off early for once and let the others close up for me tonight. Come on, Davey, let's go home.'

CHAPTER FIVE

HOME.

Lily pushed the trowel deep into the damp soil and rooted out a weed with unnecessary force as the word she had used came back to haunt her a couple of days later.

"Let's go home," she'd said to Davey, and only an hour or so later the bitter irony of her words had struck at her with a cruel force that had brought tears to her eyes.

This wasn't her home. Even though she loved everything about Belvedere House, and although, technically, it was now hers in a legal sense, Ronan having sent her the title deeds as he had promised, there was no way it could be described as being homely in any way.

If she'd had any choice in the matter, there was no way she would have stayed there, the place held so many bitter memories. It seemed that everywhere she turned she saw images of Ronan and herself in the few brief hours of their so-called 'marriage'.

She couldn't get away from her memories of the night they had been there, in the sitting room, sharing the meal in the big kitchen, and, most disturbing of all, in the huge king-size bed, their naked bodies closely entwined.

But on her marriage she had given up her small flat in town, and so if she didn't live here she had nowhere else to go. It was either Belvedere House or a settee in Hannah's home.

Davey, of course, had no idea of any of this. He believed the house was hers and had been highly impressed by its size and elegance when she had first brought him there.

'Wow, Sis!' he had exclaimed. 'This is some place you've got here! I never knew that the flower-selling business was so profitable.'

'*Selling* flowers isn't,' Lily had returned rather sharply. 'The shop may look better than the market stall I had when you left, but it's still only rented. I've only just started to make a profit

55

once the expenses and wages have been paid. If it wasn't for the flower arranging I might have gone under. Luckily, that's been more successful and brings in a fair bit.'

'Enough to pay off Ronan Guerin?' Davey had asked, though it was obvious that his heart wasn't in the question, and he had anticipated her reluctant shake of the head. 'Didn't think so.'

'We'll work something out.' She'd tried to sound encouraging. 'I'm sure he'd accept some sort of instalment plan if we put it to him.'

'I think it's way too late for that.'

'It's never too late.'

Now those words echoed in her head like a reproach, making her wish she'd never said them. How could she tell Davey it was already far too late? That Ronan had embarked on his plan of revenge and that she was tangled up in it as well as her brother? He was scared enough as it was, so how would he feel if he knew that his enemy was determined to extract far more than the financial recompense he was actually owed?

'I think you've uprooted every single weed from that bed— unless, of course, you're planning on burrowing right down to Australia. Or perhaps it's my grave that you wish you were digging.'

It was the last voice she had ever expected to hear again. The last voice she *wanted* to hear.

Or at least that was what she told herself on a very rational level. But all the rational thought in the world couldn't stop her heart from jumping right up into her throat, her pulse rate lurching into a thundering, uneven rhythm that made her head swim sickeningly as she registered the all too familiar tones that sounded behind her.

Dear God, no! she prayed. Let it not be true! Please let it be just a delusion—a fantasy. Let her have imagined it, created it out of her own fears and uncertainties. What would she do if Ronan was here, now, when Davey was back in Edgerton?

But she was clutching at straws; she knew that. There had been no mistaking that rich, deep voice, heavily laced with sardonic humour. She had no idea why Ronan had come back, but somehow she had to try to find the strength to face him.

But not just yet. Lily took a couple of much needed seconds to draw several deep, calming breaths, keeping her eyes focused on the flower-bed in front of her.

Ronan had been right, she thought inconsequentially. It was totally denuded of all the weeds that had been growing in it, and she had been in danger of digging it over so thoroughly that she had come close to uprooting all the flowers as well. It helped to concentrate her mind on the trivial fact, distracting it from the pain she knew lurked just out of sight, waiting for the moment when she turned to face the man behind her.

'Hello, Ronan,' she said carefully, ironing all emotion out of the words, as she got to her feet. Her hands were covered in mud and she wiped them down the front of her jeans, leaving a black, sticky stain that did nothing to improve their already shabby appearance. 'I didn't expect to see you again. What brings you to Yorkshire?'

'Work, amongst other things.'

He sounded slightly disconcerted, as if her reaction was not at all what he had anticipated. Lily allowed herself a small smile at the thought. If he had expected her to scream and shout, or burst into hysterical tears at the sight of him, then he was going to be bitterly disappointed. She had tried that approach on the morning after their wedding and it had got her nowhere.

If she had learned one thing from that experience it was that Ronan gave no quarter at all. Show one sign of weakness and he went straight in for the kill. She was not going to give him the satisfaction of spotting any chinks in her emotional armour. It was fastened securely round her, strong and impregnable.

'Work?'

'There are a couple of businesses for sale in Leeds. I came north to see what they're like.'

It was near enough the truth, Ronan told himself. Or half the truth at least. It didn't take into account the fact that he could quite easily have visited Leeds on a day trip if he'd wanted, or that his usual policy was to send some employee out first to see if an investment was worth considering. Only if their report was one of glowing approval did he bother to put in an appearance himself.

And it totally ignored the way that he'd been looking for just such an excuse to come north for weeks. Almost ever since he'd left Edgerton, just over a month before. At the time he couldn't shake the dust of the place from his feet fast enough, but he'd barely been back in London for twenty-four hours before he'd realised that Lily Cornwell—Lily *Guerin*—couldn't be as easily left behind.

She'd haunted him ever since; there was no other word for it. It was her face he saw every morning when he woke, projected onto the screen of his closed eyelids, and even when he opened his eyes she was still there, in his mind, no matter how hard he tried to think of something—anything—else.

And, even more disturbing, she was there last thing at night, drifting into his thoughts like some fey spirit, awakening a hunger that clutched at his loins, holding sleep at bay for long, restless hours. When he did eventually fall into a shallow doze his dreams were full of hot, voluptuous fantasies from which he awoke sweating and breathing heavily, his heart pounding, his nerves on fire.

He couldn't get her out of his mind, and in the end had been forced to admit that he couldn't go on without seeing her just once more. Perhaps that way he would be able to convince himself that she was nothing special, that with the spectacular sensuality of the one night they had spent together colouring his thoughts he had created a myth that the real woman could not live up to.

Even then he had fought against it long and hard, hating the thought that he, who had always believed himself to be a supremely discriminating and rational being, had been reduced to submitting to the control of his most basic carnal desires. But in the end he knew he had no alternative but to give in. He preferred not to think of the speed limits he had broken on his way here.

'I also thought it was the perfect opportunity to call and see how my dear wife was getting on.'

Lily steeled herself not to flinch at the black sarcasm of that 'my dear wife' as she slowly turned to face him, keeping her eyes fixed on a point somewhere beyond his right shoulder. She still couldn't bring herself to meet his gaze, knowing that the inimical blaze she would see in its indigo depths would destroy what little composure she had managed to collect for herself, leaving her floundering, speechless and totally out of her depth.

'You surprise me,' she managed stiltedly. 'I rather got the impression that you never wanted to see me again.'

'I would have *preferred* never to see you again,' Ronan returned harshly. 'What I *want* is a different matter entirely.'

Which was so inexplicable that she didn't even try to work it out. If she let it mean what she thought it might, then it didn't fit with any of Ronan's behaviour, and certainly not with everything she had learned about his character from the moment he had put his ring on her finger.

'Well, as you see, I'm fine, so now you can just get into your car and go on your way again.'

And how would she feel if he did precisely that? She tried to tell herself that it was what she wanted, that she wished he had never come, that his presence polluted the atmosphere of her home like the foul stench of some decaying matter. But deep inside she knew that it didn't come near to the truth.

She was having to fight a nasty, brutal battle with herself not to show how much he was affecting her. Her whole being hungered for the sight and sound of him, so much that she felt as if she had been starving slowly for all the weeks he had been away. She hadn't known just how much she had missed him until now, when his unexpected appearance seemed to emphasise how empty her life had been without him.

No one should have the right to look so lethally attractive, she told herself miserably, knowing that even the swift, sidelong glance she had allowed herself had already shaken her composure down to the ground. That hawk-like profile wasn't strictly handsome in the conventional sense, but when combined with those steely blue-grey eyes, the forceful, imposing height and the gloriously vibrant colour of his hair it had an impact that was nothing less than explosive.

Even casually dressed, in a loose-fitting navy suit of obviously Italian design and a crisp white polo shirt, Ronan had the sort of potent masculinity that hit home like a blow to the stomach. His devastating, purely sexual allure acted like a magnet to every woman he had ever met, and Lily could only admit weakly that even hating him as she did hadn't rendered her immune to its forceful pull.

Even the hours spent in his car on the motorway hadn't so much as creased his immaculate clothing, she thought resentfully. Beside his cool elegance she felt decidedly shabby and down at heel, in her blue flowered tee shirt and grubby jeans.

That feeling was aggravated by the way that Ronan simply stood, arms folded, subjecting her to a slow and embarrassingly thorough survey, from the top of her head to her battered, mud-encrusted shoes. Feeling uncomfortably like some insignificant and rather unpleasant specimen under a microscope, Lily shuffled uneasily from one foot to another, putting up a nervous hand to brush back a straying strand of blonde hair that had escaped from the band she had fastened around an untidy ponytail.

'You've put a streak of mud on your cheek.'

The underlying hint of laughter in Ronan's voice was almost more than she could bear. The whirling turmoil of her thoughts was made all the worse by the way he took a step forward, his hand reaching out towards her.

'No!'

Instinctively she flinched back sharply, her hands coming up defensively before her. If he touched her she would go to pieces, splintering like shattered glass.

'I was only going to offer you this.'

The clipped, cold enunciation spoke eloquently of the control he was having to impose on himself in order to bank down the fires of his anger, while the white handkerchief she now realised he had been holding out was practically flung in her face.

'You had no need to react as if you'd just come face to face with some poisonous snake about to bite. I would never harm you.'

Not physically, perhaps. In that way at least the growled reproach was justified, Lily admitted. In spite of his awesome height and strength, she had never once felt physically nervous in his presence, and had never seen that might turned against anyone weaker than him. It was the sheer emotional power he had over her that made her afraid.

'Well, aren't you even going to offer your husband a drink?' Ronan switched back to an easygoing, conversational tone with a speed that made her head spin.

No way! she wanted to fling back at him. She wanted him out of here for good—and fast, before Davey came back. The words had even formed on her lips before she forced herself to reconsider. If she seemed too keen to be rid of him, Ronan might realise something, that quick, incisive brain of his swiftly deducing just what, or rather who, she wanted to hide from him.

Davey had taken her car and driven into town earlier that afternoon. He had told her not to expect him back before teatime, and if past experience was anything to go by it would be closer to seven before he reappeared. If she was careful she could go along with what Ronan wanted and see him on his way again without him ever suspecting a thing.

'A coffee would be welcome. I've been on the road since ten.'

'One coffee...' It was all she could manage as he fell into step beside her as she headed for the kitchen.

She didn't care if she sounded ungracious. Quite frankly she felt it, and she was having to fight against the way her mind would insist on a painful awareness of how well their strides fitted together as they walked. It was impossible not to recall with bitter pain the last time they had walked side by side like this, on the way down the aisle after the black farce of their marriage.

'I have to admit that I never thought of you as a hands-on sort of gardener...'

That relaxed, casual tone shocked her to the depths of her soul. How could he be like this? How could he chat to her as easily as if they were mere acquaintances, people who had met perhaps once before?

Didn't he feel as raw inside as she did, simply at the sight of him? Didn't he know what it was like to seesaw desperately between a burning hatred that wished him a million miles away and a yearning delight that wanted to keep him here for ever?

Evidently not. In fact she was forced to wonder whether he felt anything at all.

'I couldn't imagine you getting those long, delicate fingers dirty grubbing about in the soil.'

His gesture drew Lily's eyes to her hands. A mistake, she realised, as the glint of gold where her wedding ring caught the afternoon sun had an effect like the cruel stab of a very sharp knife.

'And I certainly never saw you—'

'You never saw *me* at all!' Lily interjected sharply. 'If you had then you would never have...'

Hastily she caught herself up, gritting her teeth against the outburst that had almost escaped her. No matter how much she wanted to scream out, to fling her pain at that arrogant dark head, hurl reproach into his cold, set face, she wouldn't let herself.

To do so would be to divulge just how badly he had affected her, expose the hurt she lived with every day, the anguish of her broken heart. She wasn't prepared to let him see that. It was one dark satisfaction of his monstrous revenge that she was determined to deny him.

But Ronan wasn't prepared to let her off so easily.

'Never have...?' he questioned swiftly. 'Never have married you?'

'Never have been surprised to find me in the garden,' Lily retorted archly, grateful for the speed of thought that had got her out of an unpleasantly tight spot. 'If you'd found out more about me you would have known that my father ran a small garden centre and I got my interest in horticulture from him.'

She aimed to match his own casual tone and was delighted to find that she had managed a close approximation, even if it was light-years away from what she was really feeling.

'I love cultivating flowers and shrubs, preparing the soil, planting, feeding, nurturing—and pruning them back when necessary. It must have something of the same sort of satisfaction as looking after a child.'

'And would you be that way with a child? As a mother, would you...?'

'Oh, no, you can never control a child in quite the same way.' The way she rushed to answer the question betrayed how uneasy it had made her feel. 'All you can do is love it, care for it, and then let it go. You can hope you've taught it right and wrong, but in the end you have to set it free and let it follow its own path.'

'And would you be able to do that?' Ronan asked as they reached the kitchen. 'What if you felt they hadn't learned right from wrong, as you hoped?' There was an odd note in his voice. 'If, say, the father...'

'What is this, Ronan?'

Lily swung round from where she was filling the kettle at the sink, golden eyes blazing with a mixture of anger and distress.

'Some roundabout way of trying to find out if you left me pregnant when you walked out? Well, you needn't worry; you won't be lumbered with any unwanted consequences from that night we spent together. As I recall, you were only too careful to make sure that such a thing didn't happen—though you couched it in very different terms at the time.'

'I protected you as much as myself,' Ronan snarled, and it gave Lily a small sense of triumph to see that the normally impenetrable icy calm of his carved features no longer looked quite so assured. The thought that her words had hit home went some tiny way towards easing the hurt of her memories.

'And what, precisely, were you *protecting* me from?' she asked, pushing home her advantage while she had it.

As soon as she had asked it, she regretted the question deeply. She didn't want to know the answer, didn't want to hear him say that he had never really wanted her at all, that he had used a condom because he couldn't bear the full intimacy of making love to her without one.

'*I* didn't think I needed any such thing, remember? I thought I had married the man I loved. The man who loved me.'

'And how would you have felt if I *had* left you pregnant?' Ronan shot back. 'If I'd fathered a child on you that neither of us wanted?'

Not true! a tiny, irrational part of Lily's heart cried. If it had been Ronan's child she would have wanted it, loved it in spite of everything.

But to admit that to him would be the height of foolishness. It would be letting him know how deeply her feelings had been rooted, how much devastation he had brought to her by walking out as he had.

And besides, she was forced to wonder if in fact it was really true. Ronan's callous cruelty had fatally damaged all she had ever felt for him. He had blasted her love apart on that first morning of their marriage, shattering it into microscopic splinters that could never ever be put back into place again. One of those splinters had lodged in her heart, where it had festered, poisoning everything she now thought about him.

'So why didn't you go through with it? Did you lose your nerve?'

'Lose my nerve?' Ronan frowned his incomprehension.

'I mean, that would have been the ultimate revenge for whatever Davey's supposed to have done, wouldn't it? Leaving me stuck with a reminder of you for the rest of my life. So why didn't you do just that? Or am I supposed to believe that you do have some small saving grace, some touch of conscience? Are you claiming that your lust for retribution has its limits after all?'

'Believe it or not, it's the truth!'

Ronan sounded as if the words had had to be dragged from him with red-hot pliers, and the steel-blue eyes were smoky with some emotion she couldn't interpret. But Lily was past taking her cue from what she could see in his strong-boned face. It was as if she had tasted blood, and the rush of exultation she had experienced from knowing that she could hit back, if not enough to hurt then at least to disturb him, made her tongue run away with her.

'Not that it would have mattered, anyway,' she declared recklessly. 'After all, nowadays no one has to go through with a pregnancy they don't want. I could quite easily have rid myself of your little—leaving present.'

He'd needed that, Ronan reflected, giving himself a sharp, mental shake in order to get his thoughts back on track. If he wasn't careful, he'd find himself going soft, which could lead to all sorts of trouble. But luckily, just when he was beginning to wonder if he'd been completely in the wrong, she came out with something like this. Something that proved she was Davey's sister through and through.

'You'd have done that?' He didn't trouble to hide the disgust in his voice. 'You'd...'

Of course she would never have considered an abortion. But he thought she might, and the shock on his face was satisfaction enough for now.

'Luckily for you the question isn't relevant. I suppose I should at least be grateful to you for that.'

'Not grateful...'

He was about to add something more, but Lily didn't give him the chance. Filling a mug with coffee, she slammed it down on the table in front of him.

'The drink you ordered, sir! And I'd be *grateful*...' deliberately she laced the word with acid '...if you'd drink it quickly and be on your way.'

He ignored the mug, reaching instead for her free hand and holding it up.

'You're still wearing your wedding ring.'

'And why not?'

Lily snatched her hand away as if she'd been burned, curling it into a tight fist and hiding the gleam of gold against the blue flowered cotton of her tee shirt.

'I am still your wife in the eyes of the law at least!'

'The law only,' Ronan reminded her with brutal candour. 'But that's a matter that's almost as easily rectified as an unwanted baby.'

He greeted her gasp of shock with a small, grim smile, picking up his coffee at last, indigo eyes watching her intently over the top of the mug.

'Heard from Davey lately?'

The abrupt change of subject and the deceptively off-hand tone he used threw Lily badly off balance, as she strongly suspected they were intended to.

'D-Davey?' she hedged nervously. 'No, not a word. He...'

But some tiny movement, some uncontrolled glance towards the door had given her away. The mug slammed down onto the table again, hot brown liquid spilling everywhere.

'He's here, isn't he?' The question came with a vicious force, Ronan's eyes blazing into her shocked golden ones. 'Your bloody brother's been here all this time! Where's he hiding? Upstairs?'

CHAPTER SIX

'No...!'

It was a cry of despair, but far too late. Already Ronan had swung away from her and marched out into the hall. His long legs taking the stairs two at a time, he reached the landing before Lily had even started up, and barely paused to consider which door to open.

'Cornwell!'

Some malign instinct took him straight to Davey's room, kicking open the door in a way that was unnervingly reminiscent of every police drama she had ever seen in films or on a TV screen.

'*Cornwell*! Where the hell...!'

The dark fury and barely reined-in violence in his voice made Lily's stomach twist sickeningly. Her legs threatened to buckle underneath her but still she forced them upwards, coming to an unsteady halt at Ronan's side.

'He's been here!'

What was the point in denying it? she thought weakly. The evidence was incontrovertible, plain for anyone to see.

The bed, rumpled and unmade, could have been slept in by anyone, and the few clothes bundled onto the chair or dropped carelessly on the floor were the anonymous jeans and sweatshirts that formed a sort of uniform for anyone under twenty-five. But carefully propped up against the wall was the damning proof: Davey's beloved Gibson guitar, without which he never went anywhere.

'Where is he?'

It was low and savage, making her shiver in uncontrolled fear. She felt as if the fury that made his brilliant eyes burn almost translucent might actually shrivel her into a heap of ash where she stood.

Reaching out, Ronan captured both her wrists in a brutal grip that made her wince in distress.

'Where?'

'I—I don't...'

'Don't lie to me, damn you! I know he's been here, and he's still around somewhere. He wouldn't have left the Gibson if he didn't plan on returning. So either you tell me, or...'

'No!'

It was a gasp of shaky defiance, a hopeless attempt to come between him and her brother. She could see the hatred, the lust for vengeance burning in his eyes and it terrified her to think of it being turned on her brother. She felt like some desperate wild creature, frantically putting her own frail body between her defenceless young and some hungry predator.

And Ronan was every bit as merciless and unrelenting as the most savage jungle cat.

'I won't...'

But even as she spoke she heard the one thing she feared most. Ronan's head went back sharply as he, too, listened to the sound of her car drawing up outside, the heavy rock music Davey loved pounding out through its open windows. A moment later it was abruptly switched off.

Lily froze into immobility. Ronan's long body was taut at her side, powerful hands still gripping hers. Below them, just visible from the window, Davey slammed the car door and, all unsuspecting, headed for the house, whistling carelessly.

Oh, Davey!

Lily closed her eyes in despair at the thought of her brother walking into a trap, so blithely unaware of the presence of the dark predator who was after his blood. If she could just do something to warn him!

'Lill?' Davey was in the hall now, his voice floating up the stairwell to reach them. 'Where are you?'

Fearfully Lily met Ronan's eyes, seeing in them the danger that mixed with cruel triumph at the thought of his prey being so close.

'Call him!' he breathed in a menacing whisper. 'Get him up here.'

Lily longed to shake her head, to refuse to do any such thing, but she found herself unable to move. She could only stare into those ferocious eyes, transfixed like some small, terrified rabbit caught in the blaze of oncoming headlights.

'*Call him!*'

Suddenly the paralysis that had held her tongue frozen evaporated in a rush, and she lifted her head, swallowing hard. It was a risk, but the only thing she could do.

'Davey!' she yelled, but not in the way Ronan had commanded. Instead it was a cry of warning, an edge of panic adding a shrill emphasis to her brother's name. 'Da—'

It was all she managed. The rest of the word was cut off as a hard hand clamped over her mouth, silencing her with brutal effectiveness.

With a fierce tug of Ronan's other hand, she was yanked round to face the door, pulled hard up against the unyielding male strength of his chest, crushed so close that she could feel the throb of his heart under her cheek.

He wasn't even breathing quickly, she realised with a shiver of awareness, and the slow, steady beat of his pulse was as calm and regular as if he had just been discussing the price of fish. For all the ruthless determination that gripped him, the savage delight in finding his unsuspecting prey so near, he was physically completely cool and composed—unlike Lily herself, whose own fear and trepidation showed in her racing heart, her shallow, uneven breathing.

'Lill?'

Davey's voice was nearer now. He had mounted the stairs, reached the landing just outside the bedroom door. She couldn't just let him walk in like an innocent lamb, unaware of the vicious wolf waiting to pounce.

With one last frantic burst of strength, she kicked out hard at Ronan's leg, her mouth curling into a smile of grim satisfaction under the restraining fingers when she heard his grunt of pain as her toes made forceful contact with his ankle bone.

'Damn you!'

The words died on his lips as the door swung open, and Lily groaned in despair as her brother came into the room, stopping dead at the sight of her captor.

'Guerin!' Davey's voice was rough and hoarse, his widened eyes dark with fear.

'Well, well, if it isn't the elusive Mr Cornwell.'

Ronan's sardonic drawl sent icy shivers down Lily's spine, keeping her mouth closed even though he had released his grip on her mouth. Unable to speak, she could only try to communicate her distress with her eyes, longing to go to her brother's side, but still held prisoner by the strong arm around her waist. The silent menace in the room hung like heavy smoke, so that she found it impossible to breathe easily.

'I've been looking for you for a long time, as I'm sure you're well aware. You must have known I'd catch up with you in the end.'

'I...'

If ever Lily had wondered if her brother had exaggerated his fear of Ronan and the threat the other man posed to him, then now she was forced to admit that that was very far from the case. A million miles too far.

Davey was *terrified*. His face, already pale, was now chalk white, all the blood having ebbed from his skin, which was stretched so tight across his bones that it was almost transparent. His eyes were wide and dark with shock, his pupils dilated until there was only a thin rim of brown at their outer edge.

Lily's heart clenched in pity for him. He looked so young, so gauche, so scared; it was as if time had suddenly reversed and they were back in the terrible, bleak days after their parents' deaths. Her brother had behaved in much the same way then, she reflected unhappily, worrying her with his lack of interest in anything, his refusal to eat, his inability to sleep.

Since his return to Edgerton he had hardly eaten more than half of any meal she had put in front of him. And she knew that sleep eluded him on most nights. She had heard him thrashing about in his bed or pacing the floor in restless unease.

When he did sleep, he suffered the most appalling nightmares, often waking shouting and screaming for help, as if all the devils in hell were after him and not just this one cold-hearted fiend who now confronted him.

Lily knew only too well what images haunted those troubled

nights. They were the same as those that darkened her own sleep in times of strain. Spectres of savage flames raging through the skeleton of what had once been their home, the scent of smoke, so thick and dark it was impossible to breathe, and the scarlet flare of colour that lit up the night sky.

Knowing what he was suffering, she hadn't had the heart to question him any further about his association with Ronan and the way things had gone so terribly wrong. She had simply let him be, praying that some time of peace and quiet, much needed rest and some decent food would restore him to better health. She had even kept quiet about the money that had vanished from her purse on a couple of occasions, promising herself that she would tackle him about it when the time seemed right.

That time had never come. Well before either of them was emotionally ready, malevolent fate in the form of Ronan Guerin had invaded their lives once again, destroying all hope of any sort of peace.

And in this particular fight Davey was very definitely the weaker party, Lily reflected miserably. It was impossible not to contrast his gaunt, frail-looking form with the hard strength of the powerful male body against which she was still held tight.

'Davey...'

Calling on a strength she hadn't known she possessed, she managed to wrench herself free from Ronan's imprisoning grip, meaning to go to her brother and take him in her arms, to try to give him comfort and reassurance. But the effect of her action on Davey was the exact opposite of what she had in mind.

His head came up like that of a startled deer, his nostrils flaring in panic. Before she had time to cross the room to reach him he had whirled round, dashing out the door and down the landing, heading for the stairs. She could hear his frantic footsteps racing downwards even before she fully registered what had happened.

'Hellfire!'

Ronan's violent curse broke into her confusion, pushing her back into motion again even as her feet slowed in shock. He was just behind her, and together they followed Davey down the stairs.

As they crossed the hall Ronan's much longer stride drew

ahead, and he was well in front by the time they made it outside and onto the driveway. But even so they were too late to catch up with Davey, who evaded Ronan's grasp by a hair's breadth, leaping into Lily's car and roaring off down the drive at a speed that was positively suicidal.

'Hell and damnation!'

Ronan came to such a sudden halt that Lily, just behind him, slammed straight into his broad, hard back, knocking herself completely off balance. She would have fallen if he hadn't possessed split-second reflexes that brought him spinning round in time to catch hold of her and pull her upright again.

Uptight and distraught, Lily couldn't bear the feel of his grip on her. It reminded her too much of the imprisoning grasp of just moments before.

'Let go of me! You make my skin crawl!'

Reacting to the volatile turmoil of emotions roiling up inside her, she slapped his hands away frantically, earning herself a cynically mocking smile.

'How things have changed,' he drawled satirically. 'Time was when you couldn't get enough of my touch, when you...'

'Well, it shouldn't surprise you that I no longer feel that way!' Lily flashed at him. 'It was what you set out to achieve, after all, and you managed it only too well.'

Ronan was spoiling for a fight. Balked of his prey, he was still smarting with frustration at knowing that Cornwell had been there, within reach, and he'd slipped through the net at the last minute.

He felt wound up as tight as an astronaut who had just been counted down to the final launch only to have it aborted in the very last second, and he needed to take out his anger on someone—anyone. Lily just happened to be nearest.

'Is that a fact?' he questioned sardonically.

Stung by the way he had implied strong doubt as to the truth of her declaration, Lily welcomed the rush of anger that drove out the panic of moments before.

'An irrefutable one! Set in stone!'

She eyed him warily as he tilted his handsome head slowly on one side, subjecting her to a lazily insolent and frankly sexual appraisal that took in her flushed cheeks, over-bright eyes, and the ragged breathing that had nothing to do with the frantic race after her brother.

'And would you like to prove that?'

'No way!'

But her protest went unheeded. Once more she was caught in that painful grip and tugged towards him with a casual strength against which her feeble attempts at struggle were totally futile. She was crushed up against the potent male heat of him as she had been earlier, but this time it was so very different.

Before she had time to think, even to suspect what he might have in mind, Ronan's warm lips drifted over her face with a gentleness that was so unexpected she found herself enticed against her will. Her eyes closed, a soft, involuntary murmur of delight escaping her.

Ronan judged to the precise second the point where her defences weakened, and in that moment he captured her lips with stunning effect. From being grounded and in control, she was suddenly adrift in a blazing stratosphere, every one of her senses, every nerve, every cell shooting into orbit in the space of a single heartbeat. There was no warning, no countdown, just instant ignition, blasting her far away from any landmark she recognised and into an alien universe where she had no point of contact with anything she believed to be reality.

It was a world of pure sensation. Hungry flames licked along her veins, setting her blood alight as she kissed him back in a wild expression of need. Her whole body ached for the feel of his against it, her breasts feeling tight and heavy, yearning for the caress of those strong, warm hands. But the wildest, the most urgent sensation of all was the hungry, pulsing demand that centred at the core of her femininity.

And this time Ronan was every bit as aroused as she was, the excitement betrayed by his strong body matching hers at every point. This time his heart thundered at a heightened pace that quickened his breathing and drove a hectic colour high onto his carved cheekbones. Crushed as she was against the lean, powerful lines of his body, Lily couldn't be unaware of the most telling sign of all, the blatant physical evidence of the heated arousal that was pressed so intimately against the curve of her hip.

She shivered at the thought of the contrast between this Ronan and the man she had seen only a few minutes before. Then he had been as coldly ruthless in his determination to wreak his revenge as he now burned hotly with scorching passion.

Or did he?

The sudden shock of cold reality was like the splash of icy water in her face, making her shiver in fearful reaction. How could she have forgotten how coolly and calculatedly he had made love to her on their wedding night? Or rather, she amended with brutal realism, how cold-bloodedly he had had sex with her. She refused to honour what had passed between them with the name of love, on Ronan's part at least.

He had taken her with callous indifference to her feelings, used her for his own pleasure, and then he had discarded her without a second thought, not even looking back as he walked away. A man who was capable of doing that, a man clearly not troubled by a sensitive conscience, could perfectly well do exactly the same again if the opportunity arose. And she had been fool enough to come very close to handing him just that chance on a plate.

'And what are you proving now, sweetheart?' Ronan murmured against her cheek, his warm breath feathering across her jaw, tantalising the delicate curve of her ear. 'Are you trying to show how much you detest me? Is that it? So tell me, is your skin crawling now, my Lily? Do you truly hate my touch?'

'Yes, I do!'

It was a cry of agonised despair, ripping into the early evening air with a force that stilled the birds in the trees, silencing their busy chirping.

'Oh, God, yes, I do! I hate it! I abhor you!'

Her voice shook terribly on the words because it was only now that she realised just how clever and manipulative Ronan had been, how coldly calculating and monstrously indifferent to anything she might have suffered. How his waiting, his patience where the sexual side of their relationship was concerned, had been only a ploy designed to lull her into foolish compliance.

If he had pushed or pressurised her in any way she might have backed off, tried to put some distance between them, or at least hesitated and slowed the frantic rush to the altar they had embarked on. But instead he had been so wickedly cunning.

He had shown all the guile of a hunting wolf, homing in on her as a skilful predator singled out its prey, isolating the weakest animal from the rest of the herd. He had prowled around her, watching with cold, heartless composure, waiting with infinite patience, knowing that all he had to do was to hold back and she would do the rest. She would create her own destruction, hand herself to him, a willing sacrifice, without his having to lift a finger.

He had let her know how much he wanted her. He had made it only too plain that he was *hungry* for her, physically at least, but that for her sake he had curbed that desire, crushed it ruthlessly until she was prepared to meet him in it. He had let her think that she could set the pace at whatever speed she felt comfortable with.

And because she'd felt the same as she'd thought he did, because she'd desired him every bit as much as he had made her believe he wanted her, it had been *her* hunger that drove them on. *Her* need that had made her only too willing to agree to the earliest possible wedding date. *Her* passion that had tried to rush them into bed on their wedding night and so laid herself open to the barbaric disillusionment of his desertion the following morning.

He had walked out on her after taking her body and soul as his own and holding them captive. He had made her his loving slave that night and she doubted if she would ever break free of the chains in which she'd let him bind her weak, vulnerable heart.

'You once said you loved me,' Ronan murmured in a hatefully soft voice that whispered over her sensitised nerves, setting them jangling like an out of tune guitar.

That must have been the sort of voice the serpent had used in the Garden of Eden, Lily thought on a wave of desperation. It was no wonder it had enticed Eve so easily. Even hating Ronan as she did at this moment, it was a struggle to break free of its cajoling magic.

'*Loved* being the operative word!' she flung at him, golden eyes blazing defiance up into his darkened blue ones. 'But you destroyed all that when you walked out on me. You killed every bit of love I ever felt for you and left only emptiness in its place!'

'And now?' The question had a strangely husky intonation, as if he hadn't used his voice for some time.

'Now?'

Lily smiled with a mocking triumph that matched the one he had shown her earlier, straight into those watchful eyes.

'Now you've given me something to fill up that emptiness. Now there's no space left—my heart and my mind are full of hate for you. Total, unyielding, unchangeable, all-devouring hate. And believe me, it feels wonderful!'

'Hate?' He made the word a sound that blended frank incredulity with a strangely shaken laugh. 'So what you felt—what just happened between us—that was *hate*?'

Incensed by his open scepticism, Lily tossed her hair back, her chin coming up even higher. If he had carefully sharpened a knife before handing it to her, he couldn't have provided her with a weapon she would more happily use against him.

'You're one hell of a sexy man, Ronan,' she drawled huskily, letting her burning eyes run over him in a deliberate parody of the sensual survey to which he had subjected her a short time before. 'A real stud. But you must know that. Just as you know that we strike sparks off each other whenever we touch.'

Pausing to draw breath, she caressed him with her eyes, smiling seductively as she saw the widening of his pupils that revealed his instantaneous response. With provocative deliberation she ran her soft pink tongue along the fullness of her lower lips before she continued.

'Any fool can see that we're hot together—scorching—so I'd be a fool to even try and deny it. My mind and my heart may be repelled by you, but you turn my body on just by existing.'

Her smile grew harder as the sudden flare of something deep in those indigo eyes showed that he was well aware of her pointed reference to the way he had said almost the same thing to her on the morning after their wedding.

'What you gave me during our one brief night together was amazing—erotically exciting, sexual dynamite. It's an experience I wouldn't mind repeating over and over again. But this time with no emotion involved, no feeling at all, on either side.'

Her words were met with a silence so deep, so total it was almost shocking. All the small sounds of the day—the leaves on the trees sighing in the breeze, the faint murmur of traffic in the distance, the buzz of a bee in the honeysuckle—seemed suddenly startlingly loud, as if someone had turned the volume up to full.

Ronan simply watched her for the space of several slow, tense heartbeats, steely eyes narrowed assessingly, his dark head once more tilted to the side. Then at last he nodded slowly, a faint quirk of sardonic amusement curling his hard mouth.

'OK,' he said, his voice as slow and deliberate as the way he nodded agreement. 'If that's hatred then it suits me fine.'

And as he pulled her back to him with lazy ease time seemed to slow down almost to a halt, and all Lily could do was watch in stunned fascination as those beautifully carved lips lowered slowly to meet hers.

CHAPTER SEVEN

THIS was not what she had meant at all!

Panic ripped through Lily at the shocking realisation that her plan had gone very wrong indeed. Her behaviour had rebounded on her with quite the opposite effect to the one she had aimed for.

She had been so sure that if she showed a sexual licentiousness to match his own Ronan would be repelled by her forwardness. Either that or he would at least realise that he no longer had that particular hold over her, and let the matter drop like one very hot potato indeed.

Instead of which he seemed to have taken her declaration as a challenge. Or, even worse, he saw it as giving him carte blanche to launch into a purely physical relationship, one based solely on mutual lust and therefore free of the awkward implication and confines of any such problems as feelings, or consideration of the other.

He must have thought that all his birthdays had come at once as she'd seemed to hand him his own private fantasy on a plate. It would be just what a man like him would dream of: a woman who shared his own amoral approach to sex and who was willing to indulge it as freely and frequently as he desired.

'A real stud... Sexual dynamite...' Over and over again her own foolish words came back to haunt her, making her groan aloud at the thought that she could have been so stupidly provocative.

'My feelings exactly,' drawled Ronan, shocking her even more with the realisation that he had interpreted her response as one of sensual excitement, a lascivious anticipation she couldn't hold back from him.

'Ronan...'

But what could she say? If she panicked, pulled back and twisted out of his arms, she would have shown her story to be

78

the pack of lies it actually was. He already knew that there was no way she could stop herself from responding to him, and if she destroyed the advantage she had gained by admitting to a sexual attraction while declaring that she hated him he would know she was hiding something.

It wouldn't take that cool, incisive mind of his more than a couple of seconds to slash through the flimsy defence she had built around herself and see straight into her vulnerable heart.

Nervously she moistened the lips that panic had dried so shockingly, her head whirling with frantic, disparate thoughts. Out of the confusion she snatched at the only thing she could think of that might distract him.

'But what about Davey?'

It worked. If she had flung a bucketful of icy water in his face it couldn't have had a more dramatic effect. Ronan's proud dark head went back, blue-grey eyes narrowing sharply, the ferocity of his muttered expletive making Lily's toes curl in fearful response.

She could only pray that her brother had had enough time to get well away. The speed at which he had driven off down the drive should have taken him many miles from Edgerton by now.

'Davey.' Her brother's name was a dark-toned curse.

What the hell was he thinking of? Ronan reproved himself bitterly. It was Cornwell he really wanted; Davey who should pay for what he had done. How could he have let himself be distracted by Lily and the sexual web she spun round him so easily? It was bad enough that he had become so obsessed with her, but was he going to let her divert him from his purpose when it was all he had been able to think of for the past six months?

He had to remember Rosalie and the tragedy of her young life. God, it hurt so much to recall what had happened. He still couldn't bring himself to believe it. But that was the reason he was here in the first place. The only reason he had ever tangled with the Cornwell family at all.

But he had never expected that things would get so complicated. It had never crossed his mind that he might actually find himself attracted to Cornwell's sister, let alone that she would become an obsession with him, an itch that he just couldn't scratch. If he had even suspected the way that Lily could cloud his thinking, making him respond only to the most primitive urges, he would have steered well clear of her from the start.

'I'd actually forgotten about your rat of a brother.'

It was what she had aimed for, what she would have said she most wanted, but still she felt outrageously insulted by the speed and carelessness with which he released her. She was pushed roughly to one side as he reached into his pocket for his mobile phone, punching in a number with swift stabs of one long finger.

'Gerry?' he snapped as soon as there was a response. 'I found Cornwell but he managed to give me the slip. He—'

'What are you doing!'

In a panic Lily reached for the instrument, trying to snatch it from his hand. Ronan avoided her grasping fingers by the simple expedient of lifting it well out of reach, leaving her jumping ineffectually, her face white with nerves.

'I'm arranging for someone to take over the hunt for your brother,' he told her bluntly. 'I could kill myself for letting him get away like that. And then, of course, I was distracted...'

A quirk of one dark winged brow gave the clear message that he hadn't minded *that* part of things quite as much.

'I really am most grateful to you for reminding me of what really matters.'

Which was offensive enough to be like a physical slap in the face, leaving her gasping with shock.

'But Davey—you can't set your thugs onto him! He—'

'My *thugs*!'

Ronan's exaggerated surprise told her that she had jumped to conclusions as nightmare visions of Davey, hunted down, captured, possibly hurt, flooded her mind, depriving her of the ability to continue.

'Believe me, Gerry is no thug. But he has been helping me find your brother. I either use him again or call in the police. You tell me which course of action you favour.'

It sounded so reasonable. Almost as if he was actually offering her some sort of a choice instead of total impasse. He had her in a cleft stick, and to judge from the sardonic gleam in his eyes he was well aware of that fact.

Lily could only shake her head dispiritedly from side to side, not knowing what to think. The police would make matters official. They had rules to abide by; they had no choice. Davey wouldn't be harmed, but it was almost inevitable that he would be charged with something.

Would that charge just be breaking his contract? Or would they say that he had actually stolen all the money? That could mean a prison sentence—or would they just fine him? But of course he wouldn't be able to pay. And God alone knew what other accusations Ronan might throw at him.

'Oh, no...'

'Is that no to the police, or my friend Gerry here?' Ronan enquired, his obviously phoney and insincere note of concern setting her teeth on edge.

'You can't call in the police!'

She was past caring if her fear showed in her voice. If Davey had suffered from nightmares here, in this comfortable house, he would never survive arrest and a night or more in the cells, she knew, a shudder of horror wracking her slender body.

'Right!'

Before she had time to realise what he was doing, Ronan snapped some crisp, curt commands into his phone and switched it off again.

'Gerry will handle things.'

The colour drained from Lily's cheeks at just the thought.

'Please, no! Ronan, call off your bloodhound...!'

His harsh crack of laughter splintered the air, silencing her abruptly.

'Bloodhound indeed! Poor Gerry would be mortified by such an unflattering description. Oh, don't worry, sweetheart...'

That steely gaze raked over her distressed face, but betrayed no sign of softening at the sight of her shocked golden eyes and drawn, bloodless cheeks.

'He's very good at his job.'

If he meant that to be reassuring, he didn't succeed. In fact it had the exact opposite effect, making her legs come close to buckling beneath her. She almost felt that she would prefer her brother to face the police after all, or Ronan's cold-blooded ruthlessness, rather than this unknown tough.

'And what are you going to do while Gerry is busy with what he's so good at?'

Ronan's cold, caustic smile warned that she wasn't going to like his answer one little bit.

'Oh, I plan to stick around here for a while. Now your brother knows where you are, he's bound to try and contact you again.'

'I wouldn't be so sure of that! The last time Davey vanished it was over three years before I saw him again.'

And she'd barely got him back before she'd lost him once more. It was all Ronan's fault. Another very black mark to add to the already long list of his crimes. More coal to heap onto the fires of her hatred and keep them blazing.

'But that was before he knew you'd acquired all this wealth,' Ronan told her with malign silkiness.

He was turning away as he spoke, strolling back towards the house as if the subject was now closed, no room for further discussion.

Perhaps it was the fact that she no longer had to meet those appraising blue eyes, freeing her from their mesmerising force, that gave Lily the boost she needed to start thinking more clearly again.

Of course! Davey needed money to pay off his debts to Ronan. More money than she would ever be able to raise in her lifetime, it had seemed, but she hadn't been looking at the problem in the right light. She had been missing the obvious, but now, belatedly, it dawned on her that there *was* something she could do.

Her flattened spirits lifted sharply, her heart seeming to do a tap dance of joy inside her chest.

'Wait a minute!'

The speed with which Ronan spun round in response to her call was frankly unnerving. It was almost as if he had been waiting for her to call him back in this way.

'I want to ask you something.'

Now that she'd got his attention she found herself losing her nerve and wishing she hadn't. Her new-found courage seeped away under that cold-eyed scrutiny, his perceptible air of impatience draining her of the hope she'd stumbled on so unexpectedly.

'This house—you said it was mine. Is that true?'

'Of course.' A frown drew his dark brows together. 'Didn't you get the deeds? I...'

'Oh, yes!' Brusquely she brushed his concern aside. 'I got them. But do you mean it's truly mine?'

'Lock, stock and barrel,' was the cynically flippant response. 'You are lord—my apologies—lady of all you survey.'

'And it must be worth quite a lot of money?' Her voice lifted in hope on the question.

'A fair bit,' Ronan agreed, eyeing her curiously, as if he expected her to turn into some alien creature right before his eyes. 'But I don't see...'

'Then please won't you take it back? The house, and the allowance you promised me—everything you gave me. I know it isn't really my money, that really I'll just be giving you back something that was yours originally, but it would be something, wouldn't it?'

She tried a smile of appeal, directing it straight into those watchful dark eyes. Meeting only an inimical mask of rejection, it faded rapidly.

'It must go some way towards repaying what Davey owes you. And if you like I'll sign some sort of disclaimer, a declaration that you don't need to support me even though we're married...'

Like the smile, her voice failed her as she saw the blaze of rejection in his eyes. The look he turned on her was so filled with savage contempt it had the force of a physical blow.

'*Money!*' He enunciated the word as if it was the most obscene epithet he could conjure up, the barely controlled violence behind the syllables making Lily flinch away inside. 'You really think that *money* would compensate—would be any sort of reparation for what your brother's done? Things have gone way too far for that!'

'But they can't have!'

Lily felt as if her world had collapsed around her. Davey had told her it would be like this but she hadn't really believed him.

She had always held out some hope that Ronan would at least listen to reason. And just for a moment she thought she had seen a way to escape from the nightmare in which she found herself, something she could offer to appease that lust for vengeance that possessed him. To have it thrown back in her face like this was all the more devastating in contrast to that brief flare of optimism.

'Ronan, please…'

Just how much did this man want? Was it possible that his malevolent cruelty would not be assuaged by a simple accounting for the money Davey had caused him to lose? Davey had said that he was adding on some appalling rate of interest for every day that passed, which would mean that the original sum—huge as it was—was now building into an even greater fortune.

'It's not *enough*!' he declared inimically, rejection making his eyes burn like molten steel. Turning on his heel, he marched away from her, his powerful stride taking him out of sight in seconds, leaving her staring helplessly after him.

'No!'

Lily shook herself firmly in an attempt to clear her thoughts. She wouldn't let this happen. She couldn't give up now.

The memory of Davey's white, terrified face surfaced in her mind like a reproach, jolting her into action. She had to make Ronan listen, force him to take the house at the very least as a down payment on what was owed. What she'd do after that she had no idea, but she had to do something!

She caught up with Ronan in the sitting room, where he had pulled open the drinks cabinet and now stood with a bottle of whisky in his hand.

'I felt the need of a stiff drink,' he said as she came to a halt just inside the door. 'I hope you don't mind if I help myself.'

The overly careful politeness jarred unpleasantly with the satirical tone in which it was uttered, making Lily shift uneasily from one foot to another.

'Go ahead,' she returned awkwardly. 'It's your house.'

'I thought we'd just established that it was no such thing.' He tossed back a measure of the powerful spirit with a speed that made Lily wince. 'The house is yours and I want nothing to do with it.'

'Then I'll sell it and give you the money! Ronan, you must let me do this!'

'*Must* let you?' Ronan echoed darkly, pouring himself another drink, which Lily was relieved to see that he sipped at with considerably more restraint than the first. 'There's nothing I *must* do for you!'

'Oh, but please! I have to do something to help Davey! You have to let me help my brother!'

You have to let me help my brother!

The whisky scorched through Ronan's blood, making him feel as if he had just set light to a fast-burning fuse that led to a very large supply of dynamite, enough to blow away every chance he had of behaving rationally or reasonably.

You have to let me help my brother!

And who had been there to help Rosalie when Davey Cornwell had taken all that beauty, all that promise, that wonderful potential and destroyed it with a single careless act? Who had been there to help her mother and father, devastated by the most terrible, the most unnatural loss of all? Davey had left a trail of destruction in his wake worse than the after-effects of a tornado, and Lily wanted him to *help* her care for him!

His hand clenched around the glass he held until the knuckles showed white and he feared the fine crystal might actually splinter under the force of his grip.

'Ronan, please, just tell me what you want and I'll do it. I'll do *anything*...'

Too late, Lily realised the trap she had fallen into.

'Anything?' Ronan questioned, his voice fiendishly soft.

There was a blatantly sexual speculation in those steel-blue eyes as they slid over her taut frame, lingering with calculated insolence at the curve of her breasts in the close-fitting tee shirt before dropping to the woven leather belt that cinched her narrow waist.

'*Anything?*' he repeated, drawing out the word with a lascivious enjoyment.

Lily swallowed hard. So much for her defiant declaration earlier. And from the look on Ronan's face he had always known that he had only to call her bluff. That she wouldn't be able to follow through.

But then he laughed, a dark, brutally cynical sound that made her wince painfully deep inside.

'Not *that*,' he declared, with a venom that curdled her blood. 'I thought not. Not even for your precious Davey would you debase yourself by touching me ever again.'

If only he knew, Lily thought despondently. If only he realised the way that even now her weak body ached for the feel of his arms around her. How she yearned for the caress of his strong fingers, the warm pressure of his mouth. Her lips felt empty and lost without his against them, her breasts were tight with a primitive need that was close to pain, while the most intimate spot of all responded to even the *thought* of his touch with a sensation like the spark of a burning electric current.

'So tell me, darling,' Ronan went on, his voice sinking to a malevolent whisper, 'just what is it that Davey's got that makes him so very special?'

'Can't you see? Isn't it obvious? He's my brother—the only family I have! But of course you wouldn't understand that.'

The flash of something raw and uncontrolled in the depths of his eyes made her pulse leap in fear. For the space of a couple of frantic heartbeats, as she saw his hand tighten on the glass he still held, she actually thought he might throw it at her and her slim body tensed, ready to duck.

But then he drew a deep, ragged breath and downed the last of the whisky in an obvious effort to curb the temper that had very nearly broken from him with the force of a nuclear explosion.

'I may not have a brother to care about, as you do,' he said, each precisely controlled syllable seeming to be formed in ice, so that Lily shivered as if she could actually feel them landing on her sensitised skin. 'But that doesn't mean I'm not aware of the way that loving someone with all your heart can drive you to do something desperate, something that in a more rational frame of mind you would never even consider.' Once more he lifted the whisky bottle and unscrewed its cap.

'Are you sure you won't have one?'

'No.' Lily shook her head firmly. 'And do you really think that you should? After all, if you're driving...'

She let the rest of the sentence fall away. But if she had hoped that he would take up the hint she was sadly mistaken.

'Nice try, Lily,' Ronan drawled sardonically. 'But you're forgetting that I'm not going anywhere. I'm staying right here...'

'Davey won't be back!'

'I might have other reasons for staying.' The bottle was tilted towards the glass.

'Oh, don't!' Lily couldn't hold back any longer. 'It's barely six o'clock. You'll make yourself ill if you carry on like this.'

'Are you saying you'd care if I did?'

'Believe it or not—yes, I would!'

His expression made it clear that belief was not uppermost in his mind.

'And have you asked yourself why I might be tempted to drink myself into a stupor?'

'Would you tell me if I asked?' Lily shot back. 'Ronan, you're frightening me. You never used to be so intemperate.'

'And you weren't always so pure and prudish—apparently as virginal as the flower for which you're named!' Ronan flung at her savagely, but Lily was glad to see that he replaced the whisky bottle and moved to fling himself down in a nearby chair. 'So tell me, my sweet Lily, how much of all this has Davey told you?'

'Everything!'

'Everything?' It was a sound of pure disbelief, indigo eyes regarding her with frank scepticism.

'Yes, *everything*! All the sordid details; everything he did wrong. He confessed to it all.'

'And you still support him? You *condone* what he's done?'

If the truth were told, Lily believed that Davey had been all sorts of a fool, totally irresponsible. He needed a good kick in the pants, and something of a fright to bring home to him just how idiotically he had behaved.

What he didn't deserve was the vindictive stalking Ronan had subjected him to, the ruthless determination to take the fullest revenge possible, no matter what it cost. He hadn't earned the fear that disturbed his nights and haunted his days, turning his skin grey with panic at just the thought of Ronan Guerin.

'Be fair, Ronan.'

She came to sit in a chair opposite him, her hands open in a pleading gesture on her knees, her slim body inclined towards him. Her golden eyes begged him for understanding of her wayward brother.

'He's very young—not even twenty when you met him—and rather foolish.'

'You can say that again.' His expression was set hard as ever, no sign of any softening in his steely eyes.

'And now he feels terrible—so guilty...'

'And so he bloody well should! He deserves all that's coming to him. All that and more.'

There wasn't a trace of pity in his inimical blue-grey eyes, nothing she could appeal to and hope he might listen.

'One thing,' he went on in a very different tone. 'You haven't asked about yourself. Haven't you wondered where you fit into this?'

'Oh, that's easy.'

She wished it wasn't, but she had no alternative but to face the harsh facts. She had come to that painful conclusion in the darkness of the night, after long hours of soul-searching and questioning.

'Easy?' It had an odd inflexion, one that jarred uncomfortably with everything that had gone before.

'Oh, come on! You're not going to try and claim it was anything different! It's quite simple. You wanted to get at Davey through me. You couldn't find him but I was a sitting target, and you guessed that hurting me would punish my brother more than any attack on him.'

A weak part of her wanted to think that perhaps he might just have had a tiny twinge of conscience at what he had done. That that had been why he had given her the house and the allowance, which amounted to more money than she'd ever had in her life.

But when she looked into Ronan's face again she could see no trace of any such thing. Instead her glance seemed to recoil off the glacial hardness of his eyes, freezing in their icy glare.

'That's how it was, wasn't it? It was like some sort of vendetta where a whole family has to pay for the crimes one of them commits. Davey hurt the Guerins so his whole family is culpable. That is how you see it, isn't it?'

'Yes,' Ronan said slowly, 'that's exactly how I see it.'

So Davey really had told her everything. He found it surprisingly difficult to accept. When she'd asserted that she knew it all he had privately doubted that her brother would actually admit to what he had done, had been sure that some degree of shame would have led him to hold something back.

But it seemed that he had underestimated the family loyalty between these two. Lily not only knew of her brother's crime, she had actually done her damnedest to try and help him escape justice by offering cash to compensate for his actions. As if *money* could go any way towards filling the great aching hole in Ronan's life. He already had more than enough, and what use had all his damned wealth been when he had come up against real need?

Ronan's silence, some tiny change in his expression, made Lily wonder if perhaps he might just be reconsidering. If there was the remotest possibility he'd give her another chance, she had to take it.

'Is there nothing I can do?'

He eyed her assessingly, his eyes the colour of storm clouds.

'Would you really have sold the house?'

'Of course! And I still would if you want me to. I'd—'

She broke off nervously as Ronan suddenly got to his feet, his action bringing home to her just how tall he was, how surprisingly graceful, each muscle honed to perfection.

Once she had known what it felt like to be on the receiving end of that strength, to feel it used for positive reasons, not in any hostile way. She had felt it enclose her softly, hold her, support her. Then she had delighted in it, in the sensation of his arms around her, the knowledge that he would only ever use it *for* her, never against, and his slightest touch had made her shiver as if an electrical charge had run through every cell.

But this time her overwhelming feeling was an anxious uncertainty that set her nerves on edge, and the shudder that shook her slim body had nothing at all to do with pleasure but was tinged with genuine fear.

That sensation intensified, twisting her nerves to screaming pitch, as Ronan leaned over her chair and slid strong, square-tipped fingers under her chin. Exerting only the tiniest amount of force, he lifted it until her wide amber eyes were forced to meet the burning intensity of his.

Thirty seconds, forty, fifty slowly ticked away in total silence as he held her there, transfixed, unable to move. She was barely able to breathe, incapable of thought as he searched her face, seeming to want to probe deep into her soul to find the answer to some question that only he knew or understood. Not knowing what it was he was looking for, Lily could only keep still, meet that searching gaze with as much courage as she could muster, and wait.

At long last Ronan drew in his breath on a deep, uneven sigh and released her chin to rake one strong hand through the burnished silk of his hair.

'If you ask me, your brother doesn't deserve you,' he muttered roughly. 'Either that or you're all sorts of a fool.'

Hearing the unexpected raggedness of his words, Lily's heart gave a faint leap. It was as if she had suddenly caught sight of a tiny speck of light at the end of what had seemed like an endless, very dark tunnel. Was it possible that there was a chink in his previously impregnable armour? That he might actually listen?

She had to try one last time.

'Look, can't we work this out between us?' she pleaded. 'Can't we...?'

He was tempted. God, he was tempted! But involvement with Lily was a complication he just couldn't afford. If he let her, she would dissuade him from the path he was determined to follow. And that would mean that her brother would get off scot-free, that he would never pay for the suffering he had caused.

'There is no *we*!' His words slashed through hers like a brutal sword. 'Nothing personal. No "us"—and there never will be! This is between Davey and myself.'

'Oh, no, it isn't!'

Lily pushed herself to her feet when he would have moved away and put an end to the conversation by the simple expedient of turning his back on her. She caught hold of his arm and held him, restraining him when he would have walked away. Ronan looked down at her hand for a moment, clearly planning on shaking off her ineffectual hold, but then, surprisingly, reconsidered and simply let it lie.

'You involved me!' Her voice shook in response to her heightened emotions. 'You made it personal when you asked me to marry you!'

'That wasn't personal,' Ronan put in coldly. 'I knew who you were. You were Davey's sister and that was all that mattered.'

Lily was frankly stunned to find that she was still standing, that her legs still supported her. She felt as if they might disintegrate into tiny shards of shattered glass if she so much as tried to move. And her heart was in much the same state, so desolated by the calculated cruelty of his reply that it had splintered inside her.

'If you knew that....'

It took a monstrous effort to get the words past lips that were stiff and cold as blocks of ice. The normal flow of her blood seemed to have frozen in her veins, leaving her as cold as death.

'Then why...why did you...?'

'Why did I marry you? Or do you mean why did I make love to you?'

Hearing that emotive word, Lily lost her temper once and for all. The welcome heated rush of anger flooded through her like adrenaline, melting the ice that had clogged her emotions.

'*Love!* Don't honour what you did with the description *making love*! We both know it was no such thing!'

What had she expected? Guilt? Or sorrow? Some sign of repentance? If that was the case then she was sorely disappointed.

But she had expected *something*. Not just this blank, withdrawn silence. This total lack of any response, either conciliatory or hostile. It was as if steel shutters had suddenly slammed to behind his eyes, shutting off all sign of emotion.

'So tell me the truth. Why *did* you have sex with me? Why

not just get me to fall in love with you—marry you? Why didn't you just leave that night?'

Why had he added that final, unbearable twist of the knife to the emotional torment he had already inflicted on her?

'And make things easy for you? Oh, no, my lovely. I wasn't going to have you claiming that our marriage wasn't real, that it was never consummated. And so I made sure that it was. That way you'd have to go through the process of getting a divorce before you were free to be with anyone else.'

There was something not quite right here. Something that struck a false note, jarring badly on Lily's tightly stretched nerves. But she couldn't quite put her finger on what was worrying her, and his face gave her no help at all. His expression was still carefully blank, totally unrevealing, his eyes just slivers of glinting steel beneath thick black lashes.

'But if I have to wait for a divorce...' she tried stumblingly. 'Then so will you.'

'Yes,' Ronan agreed, the single syllable enigmatically flat and toneless. 'So will I.'

CHAPTER EIGHT

'I WARNED you that Davey wouldn't come back.'

It was almost a week now since her brother's precipitate departure from Belvedere House. A week in which Lily had slowly, unwillingly, had to adjust to having Ronan back in her life.

No, 'adjust' wasn't the right word. She hadn't *adjusted* to anything. But she had learned to cope with his presence in her home, to live with the emotional turmoil that seeing him every day inflicted on her.

And that turmoil was really her own fault. She had set out to prove how little she cared that he was back in Edgerton, but the plan had rebounded on her painfully.

When Ronan had first announced that he was staying, she had wanted to fight him tooth and nail rather than have him here, in this house that she had thought they were to share as husband and wife. She didn't care if, morally at least, he had the right to be there because he had actually bought the house in the first place. She didn't want him anywhere near her; she just couldn't bear it.

But then a very different idea had struck her, forcing her into a total rethink. If she fought Ronan as she wanted, she would be giving him the impression that she cared about him being here. If he even suspected the strain she felt at having him in the house, he would know that her feelings for him were not quite what she claimed, and that was the last thing she wanted.

So what better way to demonstrate supreme indifference than to let him move in without a word of protest? That would show him that she couldn't care less whether he came or went, that he was no longer any real part of her life.

And so she had shrugged her shoulders in a near approximation of unconcern when he had asked which room he should use.

'Does it matter? This is a monstrous great house with more than enough space. I'm sure that out of seven bedrooms you

93

could find one to use. Help yourself. You could even have the master bedroom, if you like.'

Ronan's frown told her that he knew she was referring to the room they had shared on their travesty of a wedding night.

'But I would have thought that you...'

'That I would want to sleep there?' She affected surprise at the thought. 'No chance. As a matter of fact, I wouldn't be surprised if there's something rotten under the floorboards in there. There's a singularly nasty smell hanging around the place. That's why I moved into one of the rooms that looks out over the back garden.'

But now he had been installed in the house for a week, like a hungry lion patiently waiting for his prey, and there was still no sign of Davey.

'You've frightened my brother away with your terrorist tactics, and by doing so you've ruined your own nasty little game. If Davey ever sets foot in this house again, I'll be really surprised.'

'I won't,' Ronan returned indifferently from behind the newspaper he was reading at the breakfast table in the big farmhouse kitchen. 'I think that in this matter at least I know your brother better than you do. He needs money desperately and he'll resort to anything to get it.'

'He doesn't have to come in person.'

Lily gave up all pretence at eating and reached for her coffee instead. It was impossible not to contrast Ronan's relaxed appearance, in jeans and a royal blue polo shirt, with her own stiff demeanour. Dressed as she was, in a lacy white blouse and the peach-coloured skirt of one of the tailored suits she wore to work, she was only too aware of the way that she looked like the out-of-place visitor to Belvedere House while Ronan was clearly very much at home.

'He'd only have to phone...'

'And you'd come up with the needed cash?'

The paper was lowered slowly and Ronan regarded her appraisingly over the top of it.

'You really are one hell of a soft touch.'

He sounded almost sympathetic, an unexpected softness in the words tying her nerves in knots. Seven days of living in close proximity to him hadn't done anything to lessen the potent impact of that spectacular bone structure, the compelling light eyes and forceful physique. If anything, daily exposure to his own lethal brand of sexual magnetism had only heightened her sensitivity to it, so that she was shiveringly aware of the way that even a few days' sun had brought a warm tan to the long, muscular forearms exposed by the short sleeves of his shirt.

'A soft touch *and* all sorts of a fool is what you really mean,' she snapped, fighting the unwanted tug at her heart.

Ronan lifted one winged brow in a gesture of lazy surprise.

'Did I say that?' he asked with derisive undertones of 'if the cap fits' to the words. 'But even if you are, it works to my advantage.'

'How's that?'

Lily got up from the table and moved to place her breakfast things in the dishwasher, slamming it shut again with a force that betrayed the turmoil of her feelings.

'Well, Davey obviously knows how to play you for a sucker, and so, although it looks like he's gone into hiding right now, I don't expect it will be long before he surfaces again. And when he does I'll be here.'

And he'd be only too quick to suss out any contact Davey made, Lily thought bitterly, nervously smoothing an escaping strand of golden blonde hair back into the smooth coil at the nape of her neck.

Given the choice of all the bedrooms in the house, Ronan had selected the one right next to Davey's. That way, even if her brother were to sneak in in the middle of the night, he would be sure to hear. And as he rarely left the house during the day there was no way she could prevent her brother from walking into his trap.

'I thought you said you had work to do while you were up here.'

Ronan nodded slowly. 'That's right. This trip is supposed to be business as well as...'

He let the sentence trail off and Lily found herself unable to supply a word to fill the gap. 'Pleasure' hardly fitted on any account, though she had to admit with a shiver that Ronan took a grim satisfaction in his Machiavellian waiting game.

'Some businesses you wanted to see, you said.'

'Mmm,' Ronan agreed, getting to his feet with lazy grace and stretching sensually. 'A club and a wine bar. I thought I'd go tonight and see them while they're open, so I can judge what sort of clientele they attract.'

Hastily Lily averted her eyes, not wanting to be reminded of the physical appeal of his strong body. The soft cotton of his shirt clung lovingly to the taut muscles underneath in a way that emphasised their honed power, and the well-worn jeans clung tight as a second skin on the long powerful legs and narrow waist.

'They don't sound like your usual sort of thing,' she managed jerkily.

'They're not—strictly small fry that I wouldn't normally bother with if I didn't have other concerns that would bring me north anyway. I hear they're both pretty rundown, and so they could be a bargain. If so, I'll probably snap them up.'

As he had done with Davey. The thought sent a cold, creeping sensation sneaking down Lily's spine. Would he work some other wickedly Machiavellian deal this time too? Manipulating the situation to his own advantage and leaving the owners at a loss, as he had done with her brother?

'What is it you're looking for, Ronan?' she asked acidly. 'Someone else whose life you can turn upside down?'

Her tart comment was greeted by a slow, assessing look that aggravated the already uneasy churning in the pit of her stomach.

'Davey did that all by himself, Lily,' Ronan told her with silky indifference. 'He didn't need my help in any way.'

'But he's still the one who's paying for it.'

Even though Ronan was only coming towards her to put his own plate and cup in the dishwasher, it still took all her self-control to hold her ground. Close up like this, he seemed to tower over her five foot six frame, dangerously strong and imposing.

'Do you know what you're doing to my brother? Really know, I mean? He doesn't eat, he doesn't sleep, and if he dozes off for a minute he has nightmares. I've heard him call out...'

The words caught up in her throat as Ronan lifted broad shoulders in a shrug of supreme indifference.

'Tell me about it,' he drawled sardonically. 'I know all about sleepless nights. *Excuse me!*'

Alarmed by the pointed edge to the last comment, Lily practically jumped out of his way, her eyes unwillingly drawn to the firm lines of his body as he bent to place his crockery in the machine.

The sunlight slanting through the window gilded his glorious hair, picking out the gleam of copper threaded through its darkness. It was longer now than the uncompromising crop of their wedding day, and her fingers itched to slide through it, tangling sensuously in the gleaming softness at the nape of his neck. From there they could move down to the straight, square shoulders, along the length of his spine and lower...

'What do you think?'

The question jolted her sharply out of her enticing daydream, jerking her head round until golden eyes met steely blue ones. She could only blink in confusion as she realised that Ronan now expected an answer to a question she hadn't even heard.

'Possibly,' she hedged, painfully embarrassed to find that her heated thoughts seemed to have dried her throat so that the word croaked huskily.

'I'll pick you up after work, then. The club doesn't close until—'

'Hang on a minute!' Lily shook her head to clear her thoughts of the last clinging cobwebs of voluptuous indulgence that still lingered. 'What club?'

Ronan's sigh was a masterpiece of resigned patience.

'In Leeds,' he enunciated slowly and carefully, as if speaking to a slow-witted child. 'The one I'm going to tonight. The one you've agreed to go to with me.'

'I've done no such thing!'

Too late she realised that this had been the question she hadn't heard. Ronan had taken her abstracted murmur as agreement to his proposal that she accompany him.

'I don't know what makes you think I'd want to go anywhere with you. I'd rather die!'

The little shudder of repugnance she gave was the last straw as far as Ronan was concerned. For the past week he had fought to control the force of his physical feelings for Lily, with all the success of someone trying vainly to put a lid on a volcano that was about to erupt. He might as well try to hold back the flowing tide of red-hot lava with a child's fishing net.

After several long, sleepless nights, and even longer days, trying to ignore the violent way his body reacted to just the sight of her, the scent of her skin, the sound of her voice, what little patience he had was stretched to breaking point. He wanted her so much that it hurt even to think about it, and he no longer cared about the possible consequences if he gave in to that need.

And Lily herself was no help. After that blunt declaration about the way she felt about him, she seemed to have retreated into her shell like some small hermit crab. But time and time again he had caught her looking at him when she didn't think she was observed, and because he felt the same way he had instantly recognised the hunger in her eyes for what it was.

There was no way they could deny their passion for each other. It played around them like forked lightning in an electrical storm, striking sparks in the air and building up an atmosphere that grew more and more oppressive with each second they spent in each other's company.

And he for one had had enough. Something had to happen to ease the tension between them or the resulting explosion would have the force of a nuclear bomb. Except that this time the resulting devastation would be emotional rather than physical.

'Fine.'

His immediate, unconcerned acceptance of her refusal, the way he simply ignored her snappish indignation was just too much for Lily. Perversely they had the exact opposite effect to what she had expected, making her pause briefly and reconsider, even allowing a faint thread of regret to slide into her thoughts.

'I'll go on my own.'

'And what if Davey comes back?'

What was she doing? Reminding him of why he was here would only make him change his mind, abandon the trip to Leeds and return to his post as watchdog, waiting for her brother to reappear.

But to her surprise Ronan appeared untroubled by the thought. 'I'll take a chance on that. After all, Gerry is still on his trail, and your damn brother isn't the only reason I'm up here.'

'No, you hope to make even more money by getting your claws into other victims who can't see through you.' She flung the words with scathing force into his dark, controlled face.

'That as well,' Ronan confirmed carelessly. 'But there are more personal reasons. We are still man and wife,' he elucidated as she stared in blank incomprehension.

'And we both know that means nothing at all!'

A slow, dangerous smile curled Ronan's sensual mouth in response to her furious outburst. It was positively fiendish, almost sensuous in its predatory anticipation, and he took a slow, deliberate step closer, making Lily stiffen in instinctive rejection.

'Perhaps,' he murmured smoothly, his caressing tone making her toes curl in uncontrollable response inside her elegant high-heeled shoes. 'But it is legal, my darling Lily. All above board, signed and sealed, and...'

That purring voice dropped an octave, became positively sinful in its carnal enjoyment.

'Very definitely consummated. You're my wife; you bear my name.'

'A convenience, nothing more! I had already arranged to have everything changed before our parody of a marriage, and I really couldn't be bothered changing it back again.'

The uneven breathlessness of her voice destroyed the image of indifference she was aiming for, but she couldn't bring herself to care. Her heart had already leapt into overdrive, sending hot pulses of awareness through her body. Simply by moving close to her he could spark off this unwanted reaction in every cell, and there was no way she could hide it.

'A convenience,' Ronan echoed softly. 'Certainly it is *very* convenient...'

He used the low, smoky voice to weave a lingering spell around her senses, enticing each one awake to the sight, the sound, the arousing, intensely personal scent of his strong body.

He was so very close now that she felt that if she let herself lick her parched lips she would actually taste him on them, relishing the salty tang of his skin as she had done in their most intimate moments of lovemaking.

'Because now we can take up from where we left off.'

'Never!'

The rejection tangled in her throat, almost choking her as his hand brushed her cheek very gently. Slow, sensuous fingers slid along the delicate line of her jaw, down the slender column of her throat, insinuating themselves into the lace-edged neck of her blouse.

'I—don't want...'

'Liar,' he reproved softly, those exploring fingers moving deeper under the white silk, his arrogant assumption that they had a perfect right to do so making her tremble as she struggled with an inner conflict that threatened to tear her mind in two.

She *wanted* this! Wanted it with a need that made her ache with heated excitement. Physically she was burning up with a hunger that had been building since that first devastating experience of his lovemaking on their wedding night.

At some point during those long, glorious, passion-filled hours, Ronan had discovered the door to the deep well of sensuality that lay at the core of her being, undiscovered until then, but now impossible to conceal ever again. He had unlocked that door that night, and when he left he had taken the key with him so that she could never hope to close it against him even if she tried. The hunger and the need that he had awoken in her then could only ever be truly appeased by one man—this man.

'I don't...' she tried again, even less convincingly this time.

And Ronan knew it. That predatory smile surfaced again and his other hand tangled in her hair, destroying the sleek style as the pins she had used to fasten it were pulled loose and tossed to the floor. Tugging softly on the golden strands that coiled around his long fingers, he pulled her head back until her stormy amber gaze met his coolly appraising stare.

'I don't believe you, my darling.' His total calm, his lofty assurance were fiendish in their complete lack of emotion.

'What there was between us that night was like a bushfire

raging wildly out of control. It could never be extinguished by anything as trifling and insignificant as rational thought. It's all still there, bubbling just under the surface, needing nothing more than a touch...a kiss...'

That proud dark head bent slightly, as if he would kiss her, his smile twisting, growing grim as she jerked her head away. She couldn't hold back a wince of pain as the unwary movement wrenched at the golden strands of hair he still held.

'...to start it up again. If we let it loose it may burn us up, but if we try to keep it in check we'll go mad. So why don't we take advantage of something that could be so spectacular, my lovely wife? Why not admit that we both *want* this? That we're both hungry, both crazy...'

'Won't—won't that delay your divorce from me?' Lily managed to croak, clutching at the one straw she could think of, the one thing that might persuade him to release her from this sensual torment. If he didn't set her free then she was lost. There was no way she could fight the overwhelming force of her need for him any longer.

To her horrified consternation her question had nothing like the effect she had anticipated. Instead, Ronan's smile grew wider and his eyes darkened perceptibly, taking on the shadowy tones of a rain-laden sky.

'Who says I even want a divorce? The brief taste I had of married life simply whetted my appetite for more. I'd like to take things further—so much further.'

Briefly Lily closed her eyes against the husky enchantment his words wove around her beleaguered senses. But she opened them again in a rush when she discovered that her self-imposed blindness only added to the highly charged sensations she was experiencing.

Being unable to see enhanced her awareness of Ronan's physical presence, infinitely heightening her sensitivity to the slightest touch. She heard even the faint sound of his breathing with a new clarity, the sound of his heartbeat assailing her ears like thunder. And inhaling the clean scent of his body brought her a degree of pleasure that was almost a pain.

'You'd just be using me for your own selfish ends!'

He didn't deny it. He didn't even look the slightest bit abashed at her sharp accusation. On the contrary, his expression was fiendishly amused, pure devil-cat-who-got-the-cream as he nodded a hatefully smiling agreement.

'And you me,' he returned imperturbably. 'It's true, isn't it?' The question cut across her attempt to voice a heated protest. 'You claimed you didn't love me any more.'

I lied! A desolate voice cried in the darkness of Lily's mind. Dear God, I *lied*! I still love you and I always will. I never stopped loving you—I can't! It would be like dying!

'So your love died, but you can't claim that passion went with it,' Ronan continued inexorably, his stunning features stamped with ruthless determination. 'You can't say that you don't want me any more because that would be a lie, and we both know it. It's written in your face, in your eyes. You can't deny the way your body responds to me, the hunger that you feel, the way...'

Those long fingers rested against the pulse point at the base of her neck, just under the delicate lace of her collar, and Ronan's cruelly beautiful mouth curled in dark triumph at what he felt there.

'The way your heart flutters like a wild bird when I touch you. But you say you don't love me, so for you it would be no more or less than what you've just accused me of wanting. It would be passion without feeling, physical pleasure without emotion...'

He had released her hair now, those strong, sure hands moving to tip her head upwards, lifting her mouth towards his as his head came down with deadly intent.

'But, oh, my lovely Lily...' It was a thickened whisper against her lips. '*What* passion...what enchantment...what burning heat of pleasure. And what *ecstasy* would come from it.'

He punctuated each whispered phrase with a kiss, unbearably brief, heartbreakingly gentle. Kisses that tore at her heart with their lying promises of love, of feelings he could never possess. And in his dark eyes smouldered a burning need, a hunger that matched the one that had reduced her to a mutely trembling wreck in his bruising grasp.

'And if *I* don't object to being used as a sex object in this way, then why should you complain? We're both adults, both equals in desire...'

She was lost. Lily's moan of surrender admitted as much, a moan she couldn't have held back if she tried. But she didn't try. She was beyond being able to control herself, beyond struggling against feelings that had all the force of a tidal wave breaking over her head as she went down for the third time.

She could do nothing but give herself up to the practised caress of his lips, the confident, knowing touch of those strong but stunningly gentle hands. She could only murmur her delight as long, warm fingers cupped the weight of her breasts, the heat of his palms burning through to the sensitive skin beneath the silk.

In a haze of delight she felt herself lifted off her feet and half walked, half carried through into the lounge. There he lowered her onto the green velvet cushions of the settee, his long, lean body easing down beside her and pulling her close to him.

'This is how it should be between us, how it's always been. How it can be again if you don't fight it. You know it's what you want, my Lily, you remember how it was that night. So don't struggle, don't think, just lie back and enjoy it.'

Remember! The word slashed through the golden waves that were drowning her thoughts with the force of a cruel blade, shattering the foolish sensual delusion that had held her captive.

Remember! In the dark, echoing chasms that her mind had become she could hear Ronan's voice saying that word before, in a very different way.

On their wedding night, his voice rough with dark satisfaction as he branded her with the mark of his sexual possession, he had told her never to forget. 'Remember!' he had said. 'Remember this...!'

And how could she have forgotten? How could she have let the way he had behaved then be wiped from her mind, driven away under the force of the sensual assault he had subjected her to? How could she forget the appalling disillusionment that had struck at her at the end of that deluded night, the dreadful reality that had intruded into her foolish dreams of happiness, shattering them once and for all?

'No!'

In an agony of despair she wrenched her mouth away from the sinful temptation of Ronan's kisses, her hands pushing frantically and ineffectually at the hard wall of his chest in a vain attempt to distance herself from him.

'Enjoy it!' The words were torn from an aching throat. '*Enjoy it!* Oh, yes, you can make me take pleasure from what you're doing *physically*; we both know that! But we also both know that with nothing else there, no sort of feeling in our hearts, it would be nothing more than just scratching an itch—an act of bestial lust, lower than the level of animals, because we are capable of so much more.'

Her breath seemed to sear into lungs that were suddenly agonisingly raw with tension, each breath she took a painful effort. But she was aware of the fact that Ronan had frozen at her side, ceasing the unrelenting assault on her senses.

'Of course you can work on my *body*. I couldn't deny that if I tried...'

The conflict between her emotional need to stop him and the wanton urging of her body to let things continue made her voice shake with tension. Every one of her hypersensitive nerves was beginning to scream in protest at the abrupt denial of the pleasure they had been feeling, the fulfilment they had been yearning towards, so that she ached all over, as if her skin was a mass of bruises.

'You can kiss me, arouse me, bring me to a point where I can no longer *think*, where my physical needs override the emotional ones. Where I'm no longer a human being, but just a *hungry, crazy...*' deliberately she echoed his own words, lacing them with acid '...heap of nerves and hormones. Oh, yes, you can make me *enjoy* this!'

She heard Ronan's breath hiss in between clenched teeth, but she didn't dare to look up into the dark face that was only inches away from her own for fear of what she might see there.

'But be very sure of one thing, Ronan, if this is the way you plan to go. Know that the more I enjoy *mating* with you, the more I will detest you afterwards. If you use me as a sex object, and by doing so make me use you for the same purpose, then I will hate you till the day I die for reducing me to something so low!'

Her impassioned words died away into a silence so profound, so heavy with danger that she could almost feel it closing around her, filling her lungs, threatening to choke off her breathing. But then at last Ronan stirred, raking rough hands through his hair, the gesture breaking the unnerving tension that had held him so unnaturally still.

'It might almost be worth it,' he muttered roughly.

The words made Lily tense fearfully, wide, shocked golden eyes going to his face and finding it closed and shuttered against her. But as their eyes locked and clashed his mood changed again, and he swore in a darkly eloquent stream under his breath.

'Damn you to hell, Lily!' he flung at her as he jack-knifed off the settee and away from her in a violent movement that took him halfway across the room. 'You really know how to go for the jugular! You didn't need to make me feel like the lowest form of life that has just crawled out of the primeval slime—a simple no would have sufficed.'

'Would it?'

The look he threw her was so black, so full of dark contempt that he didn't have to say a single word to expand on his feelings. And this time it was Lily's turn to feel like the lowest form of life—not a sensation she liked at all.

'Well, I'll remember that in future,' she managed, levering herself into an upright position and getting to her feet with as much dignity as she could manage, with her blouse gaping open widely and her skirt pushed up to somewhere around her hips.

'See that you do.'

They were like two hostile cats, Ronan thought wryly. Each eyeing the other warily, heads up, shoulders stiff with hostility. He could almost see the hairs on the back of her neck lifted in tense aggression. She didn't want to be the first to look away, trying to restore order to her disordered clothing without a single downward glance, and yet she didn't know how to break the silent impasse.

If it came to that, neither did he. Now that the explosive maelstrom of feelings that had boiled up in him at her rejection was slowly coming back under his control he found himself veering from one emotion to another without knowing which he would finally settle on.

Frustration was uppermost, burning, aching frustration that made his whole body feel as if he'd gone ten rounds with a prize-fighter. And mixed in with that was an anger that at first had threatened to get away from him, slipping right out of his control. But the problem was that he didn't know whether his wrath was aimed at Lily, himself, or the whole complicated situation in which they found themselves.

Damn Davey Cornwell to hell! His mind fixed on the one sure person he knew he could blame for his predicament. If Lily weren't Davey's sister then things would have been quite different between them. When his mind threw at him the unwelcome fact that if Lily hadn't been Davey's sister then they would never have met in the first place, he pushed it aside impatiently. He didn't want to remember that he had gone to the Hodgson wedding with the sole purpose of meeting her.

So was he going to give up? Accept her refusal once and for all?

His dark-eyed gaze went back to Lily, seeing the tumbled glory of her blonde hair, the full softness of her lips, still faintly swollen from his kisses.

He wanted more of those kisses, more of the feel of her skin against his, more—hell, he wanted more of everything! More of the passion they had shared on their wedding night. No way was he going to give up! She didn't get away that easily!

But he wanted her willing. And he certainly wasn't prepared to tolerate her describing his lovemaking as something bestial. When they next slept together—and they would sleep together, he had no doubt of that—she would come to his bed of her own accord, because she wanted to, because she couldn't damn well help herself.

But that required a change of tactics. There was more than one way to skin this particular cat, though right now Lily looked more like a small, furious kitten than a full-grown animal. Softly, softly was the way he'd handle it from now on.

'I take it that no goes for the trip to Leeds as well?'

Lily eyed him suspiciously, frankly confounded by the sudden gentling of his voice, the megawatt brilliance of the smile he had turned on her. Just what had brought about this change of tack?

She had opened her mouth to say, yes, that was exactly what she meant, when a sudden thought made her reconsider.

Ronan was going to Leeds to see some properties. If he liked them, he would snap them up, just as he had done with Davey. Earlier she had feared that the owners might end up in the same snare as her brother had, or worse, and she'd wished there was something she could do to prevent it.

But there *was* something she could do. If she went along tonight she could warn them, or at least try to get them to stand up for their rights. It was just possible she could stop them from doing anything foolish.

'No,' she said impetuously, only realising when she saw his change of expression that he had interpreted her answer as meaning that, no, she wasn't going with him.

'I mean, no, that's not my answer!' she corrected hastily. 'To the trip to Leeds. I... Oh, what I'm trying to say is that, yes, I'll come.'

If he had surprised her earlier, then now it was her turn to take him aback. Ronan blinked hard just once, but a moment later he had adjusted again.

'May I ask why?'

Lily shrugged slender shoulders with what she hoped was just the right degree of careless insouciance.

'I haven't been anywhere in ages. Leeds wouldn't be my first choice, but if that's all you're offering, I'd be glad of a night out.'

And if he wanted to add 'even with you', then that was fine with her.

'Your gracious acceptance overwhelms me.' The words were strangely stiff, in spite of their undercurrent of pointed satire. 'We'll leave here at seven, if that suits you.'

For the first time since he had reappeared in her life a week earlier, Lily actually felt as if she had gained, if not the upper hand, then at least some degree of control over the situation. She had reasserted herself, gained a foothold that was rather more secure than before. The relief that feeling brought was so intense that she flashed a wide, bright smile straight into his unyielding face.

'That'll suit me fine,' she told him cheerfully.

It was only much later, with hindsight, that she had cause to wonder just what had put the gleam of satisfaction into his indigo eyes that she spotted just before he turned away.

CHAPTER NINE

'HAVING fun?'

The question was a warm murmur in Lily's ear. Ronan's dark head was bent close to hers, the heat of his breath caressing her skin.

'Mmm....'

She managed an inarticulate murmur that did nothing to express the way she was feeling. Instead it was more a response to his nearness, the way his powerful body brushed against hers as he leaned so close, the faint, musky scent of his aftershave and the sensual slide of his silky hair across her cheek as he spoke.

But she *was* having fun. That was the most surprising thing about the evening so far. She had never expected to enjoy herself, seeing the trip as a duty rather than a pleasure, but in fact she had. From the moment she had appeared at the foot of the stairs, precisely at seven as arranged, there seemed to have been something special about the night.

She had spent a long time considering what to wear, eventually settling on a dusky rose-coloured slip dress, the skirt of which came to just above her knees. Silver drops sparkled in her ears and a matching necklet circled her slender throat. Her high-heeled sandals gave her extra confidence, making her tall enough to be able to meet Ronan's blue-grey gaze head-on when she'd looked into his face to see what effect her appearance had on him.

What she had seen there both thrilled and terrified her. Sensual approval blazed unconcealed in the dark pools of his eyes edged by thick, dark lashes, his pupils widening until there was nothing but a thread of colour at their outer edge.

'Very nice,' he'd drawled softly, the husky note in the words catching on her nerves and making her pull in her breath in a small, shaky gasp.

'You're not so bad yourself.'

She'd forced herself to match the frankly sexual appraisal in both his look and his voice as she'd let her gaze run over the sleek, toned lines of his body in the breathtakingly elegant Italian-styled silver-grey suit and crisp white shirt. Her heart had turned over in instinctive reaction as she'd allowed herself just one moment of purely physical response to the man before her.

With the last of the evening sunlight gilding his glossy hair, turning the copper strands into streaks of bronze flame and highlighting the masculine beauty of his bone structure, he was very definitely the irresistible force personified. And, no matter how hard she tried to be the appropriate immovable object, deep down inside it just wasn't working. That dark magnetism of his still tugged at every one of her senses, warning her that she was only too vulnerable to its appeal. She might have won a major battle, but there was still a great deal of the war to go.

And if she had ever had any doubt about that, then it was brought home to her now, with Ronan's lean body so close, his indigo gaze fixed on her face and a strange half-smile playing around his expressive mouth.

One long hand rested on the bare skin of her shoulder, reminding her of how it had felt to have those warm fingers on other, much more intimate parts of her body, so that a shiver of response ran down her spine. That smile made her skin tingle, as if she was affected by pins and needles all over her body, an electric current of excitement filling her with a restlessness she could neither subdue nor ignore.

She couldn't stay still any longer. She had to do something—anything! It was either that or reach for him, wind her arms around his narrow waist, bring her lips to his and kiss him stupid.

'Let's dance some more!'

'We've only just stopped!' It was a groan of protest. 'I need a drink.'

'You're chicken!'

She spoke sharply to drown out the sensual temptation her thoughts were offering. Not giving herself a chance to think, she grabbed at his hands, curling her fingers around their hard strength.

'Come on! We can't sit here all night, propping up the bar! I came out to enjoy myself!'

With a tug she pulled him towards the small square of wood that passed for the dance floor, manoeuvring her way into its already very crowded centre. Once there, she launched herself into a flurry of rhythmic movement that had more to do with the need to suppress the wanton direction of her thoughts than any response to the beat of the music.

But here, too, Ronan surprised her. For a big man, he danced with a natural grace and a total lack of inhibition that soon had her smiling in delighted response and adjusting her wild gyrations to something more appropriate and far more enjoyable.

Their steps matched perfectly, their bodies coming close, touching briefly and swinging away again in an expressive response to the sound of guitars and drum from the stage. Unable to suppress her feelings, Lily tapped her feet and clicked her fingers excitedly, laughing up into Ronan's smiling eyes.

'They're good!'

She nodded towards the band, crammed onto the tiny rostrum. Rake-thin and crop-haired, the four young men, barely more than boys, were an unimposing sight in themselves, but their music was fresh and exciting, perfect for a night like this.

'Perhaps you should give them a regular spot here if you decide to buy the place.'

She fought to pitch her voice above the pounding beat, then gasped as he caught her hand and swung her close.

'Do you think I should?' he asked, his lips once more almost touching her ear, so that she stiffened in nervous reaction.

'Well, I like them—but what do I know about it?'

'You're Davey's sister. You should know something. Surely he can't be the only one with any musical talent in your family.'

He shouldn't have mentioned Davey's name. As soon as he did so the bubble of delight that had enclosed her burst with an unwelcome pop. The memory of her brother and his shattered hopes, the dreams he had had since childhood, forced itself into her thoughts, bringing her down to earth with a bump.

And with that cold realism came the unwanted recollection of the harsh, impossible conditions Ronan had imposed on her brother, driving him to despair and the ruinous situation in which he now found himself. Her mood changed abruptly, her feet stilling as if she had suddenly had iron weights fastened to them. She stood unmoving in the middle of the dance floor, oblivious to the whirling figures around her.

Fool! Ronan berated himself. You bloody stupid fool! Why did you have to go and mention Davey's name? Just when she was beginning to relax, to enjoy herself, you had to go and remind her...

Being with Lily was like being on an emotional switchback ride, going up one moment, only to plunge right down the next. But if ever he was tempted to give up, he only had to remember how she'd looked when she was dancing. Just the thought of her smile, the sensual way she'd moved to the music was enough to spark off the gnawing hunger that was always so very close to the surface these days.

But then he looked into Lily's stiff face, seeing the bitter reproach in her eyes, and his mood changed abruptly.

'Yes, I'm Davey's sister, and as such I should warn those kids not to have anything to do with you. You wouldn't just want their music—their talent—you'd want everything they've got. Their lives, their blood—their *souls*!'

'Not theirs, only Davey's,' Ronan returned coolly, and the icy conviction in his voice, in those suddenly silvery eyes, left her in no doubt that he meant exactly what he said.

The dark seam of menace that ran through his words sent a cold trickle of fear sliding over the heated skin of her back, so that she shuddered convulsively. She had to get right away from him now or be violently sick, right here in the middle of the dance floor.

'I—must just go and powder my nose,' she gasped unevenly, escaping before her mind could fully register the scornful curl of his lips at her transparent excuse.

In the privacy of the Ladies' she splashed cold water on her face, ran it over her wrists in an attempt to cool her unnaturally racing pulse. She should never have come here! She hated Ronan, hated and loved him in a volatile combination that threatened to explode right in her face if she allowed one more spark of that deadly excitement he could create in her anywhere near it.

She hated him more than ever now. Because that one brief respite from her feelings that she'd had tonight had made it all the more impossible to handle things when they went back to normal, as they inevitably must. She felt like Cinderella once the clock had struck twelve. But what made matters worse was the fact that it wasn't just her coach and horses that had changed back into a pumpkin and a pair of rodents. Prince Charming himself had turned out to be the biggest rat of them all.

She lingered in her refuge for as long as she dared, only emerging when she was sure that if she lingered a moment more Ronan was perfectly capable of breaking down the door and dragging her out by force. As it was, she fully expected him to be waiting outside to pounce on her as soon as she emerged, and so she was frankly surprised to see him standing calmly at the bar.

'I thought you'd climbed out of a window and escaped,' he said as she reached him, shocking her with the accuracy with which he had guessed at the craven thought that had passed through her mind. 'Either that or you'd locked yourself in.'

'I...' She hunted for a suitably quelling reply, but Ronan wasn't listening.

'We're moving on,' he said abruptly. 'Time for a change of scene.'

Time for her to stand up to him, Lily decided, and drew herself up to her full five feet six, her chin lifting determinedly.

'And what if I don't want to?'

'You want to stay here?'

A contemptuous wave of his hand encompassed the cramped dance floor, crammed as tight as a tin of sardines, the grubby décor and smoky atmosphere. It seemed that everyone in the room was more than two or three sheets to the wind.

As Lily looked around one of a bunch of young men at the far end of the bar winked at her lewdly, lifting his glass in a lascivious toast. Mercifully the music was loud enough to obliterate what was obviously an obscene suggestion that he mouthed in her direction.

'I...' she began again, but never managed to complete the sentence.

Ronan's hand clamped around her wrist with a force that made her wince in discomfort, and she was yanked away, forced to stumble after him as he strode from the room. His long, powerful legs covered the ground so fast that she had to trot awkwardly in order to keep up with him. It was either that or be dragged, uncaring, in his forceful wake.

'Let go of me, you caveman!'

She wasn't sure whether he actually heard her or not, only that he came to such a sudden halt that she cannoned into his broad back, knocking all the breath from her lungs.

'Let me go!' she tried again when she had recovered, using her free hand to pound against the arm that held her, feeling the hard power of muscle under the fine silk of his jacket. 'How dare you treat me like this? Like some primitive Neanderthal dragging his woman off by the hair!'

'If I'd known that was what you preferred...'

Ronan was deliberately needling her, she was sure. Though she didn't like the way the hand that wasn't holding hers moved to her head, brushing very softly against the golden fall of hair down her back. Only when her breath hissed inwards sharply did he release her with a mocking smile.

'I wanted you out of there,' he stated calmly. 'I had no intention of standing by and letting those—yobs...' the word was chosen with cold precision, his eyes glittering like ice in the moonlight '...make advances to my wife.'

'Your wife!' Lily exploded. 'I'm not your wife! I...'

Words failed her as Ronan snatched up her left hand and held it so that the wide gold band he had placed on it over a month before gleamed in the light of an overhead street lamp.

'You wear my ring,' he stated, with such unruffled self-assurance that it short-circuited Lily's brain, destroying her already shaky grip on her temper altogether.

'I might as well wear your brand!' she flung at him. 'This—'

A jerky tug pulled the ring from her finger and she held it up between them.

'This isn't a marriage band, a sign of love and a promise of commitment! It's nothing more than an instrument of torture. You might as well have given me a slave's collar, like those forced on prisoners long ago by brutal oppressors who wanted only to possess and destroy, who didn't give a damn about whether their property had any feelings! Here...'

She thrust it at him, pushing it almost into his face.

'Take it back! It would contaminate me to wear it any longer!'

Ronan made no move to take the ring from her, regarding her stonily through eyes that seemed to be the only living part of a face that was as set and unyielding as if it was carved from marble. His long body remained totally motionless too, frozen into silent immobility.

'No? Then let me show you what I think of it!'

Whirling round, she faced the canal that ran alongside the car park, its water black and menacing in the light of the moon. With a wordless cry she flung the ring with all her strength and watched it curve high in the air before hurtling down towards the mirror-smooth surface. Her feelings when she heard the faint splash of its landing were such a tangle of painful contradictions that they made her feel as if her heart was being twisted cruelly by some powerful, brutal hand.

For one appalling moment she thought that Ronan was going to react violently to her dramatic gesture. Every muscle in his already taut frame tightened even more, his hands clenching as his eyes blazed down into hers. Lily nerved herself for the explosion she felt sure must come, and didn't quite know how to react when instead he drew in a deep breath and let it out again with agonising slowness.

'For better, for worse,' he muttered enigmatically, leaving Lily incapable of decoding the dark undercurrents that took the words to a point light-years away from the way they would be spoken in a wedding ceremony.

'Oh, very definitely for worse!' she spat at him. 'I don't see how things could deteriorate any further.'

'And so you want to go home?'

The question surprised her so much that for a couple of seconds she couldn't get her brain working well enough to consider it.

Home. He meant go back to Belvedere House, to that beautiful building where she had once thought she would live with him as his wife.

Home. She would be there with Ronan in the silence of the night, would have to go to bed once more, knowing that he was just along the corridor. And as on every other night this week she would hear the small, intimate sounds of him preparing for bed, the opening of a door, the rush of the shower...

Suddenly the noisy anonymity of the club seemed infinitely preferable.

'I thought you came out to work.'

She was proud of her coolly indifferent delivery, thankful that she had given away nothing of what it had cost her to pitch it that way.

'Don't let me hold you back. After all, the night is still young.'

'You want to go on?'

'I don't want to go back.' Carefully she avoided that emotive word 'home'. 'And who knows? Now that I'm no longer branded as your possession...'

Provocatively she waved her ringless hand under his nose, concentrating on the flare of fury in his shadowed eyes so that she wouldn't have to think about the pang of distress that ripped through her at the sight of her naked finger.

'At the next place I might just meet someone who knows how to give a girl a good time!'

The place he took her to was very different from the club they'd just left. Lily felt that she had never been so glad to see anywhere as she was to find herself safely inside the small, old-fashioned bar, where the atmosphere was one of quiet relaxation in contrast to the frenetic excitement of the club they had first visited.

They reached it after a brief, unpleasant, deeply uncomfortable ride. Ronan hadn't spoken a single word to her throughout the journey, and he had driven the Mercedes at a speed that expressed the inner fury he was keeping under ruthless control. At times Lily had been genuinely afraid for her life, thankful that Ronan's skilful handling of the powerful vehicle had kept them from any sort of an accident.

'Drink?' he enquired curtly once they were inside.

'Mineral water, please.'

She would have liked to ask for a large brandy to settle her nerves after the nightmare drive through the dark streets, but refused to let Ronan know that he had rattled her in any way.

He was still at the bar when Lily felt someone touch her gently on the elbow. Turning sharply, she saw a young woman standing at her side. Tall and voluptuously curved, with long dark hair, she was perhaps twenty-two or three, her smile nervous and unsure.

'Excuse me, but are you with Mr Guerin?'

At Lily's puzzled nod, her smile grew a little more confident. 'I'm Allie Gordon. My father owns this place, with my mother.'

'I thought it must be a family business. It has that sort of a feel.'

It had struck her right from the start. The room might be dowdy and in need of redecoration, but the wine bar had a friendly, relaxed atmosphere that had appealed straight away.

'I'm surprised your father wants to sell.'

'Oh, he doesn't *want* to, but it has to be done.' There were deep shadows in the wide blue eyes. 'That's why I'm here, to talk to him about it. You see, my Dad's ill—we just found out he has Alzheimer's. He's going to need constant care, and Mum can't look after him and run this place as well. Besides, we'll need the money.'

Ronan was coming back to the table, glasses in his hand. Lily had barely time to murmur, 'I'll see what I can do,' before Allie had hurried off again.

So what did she do now? How could she persuade Ronan to buy the wine bar at a price that would give the Gordons the money they obviously needed?

'Well, what do you think?' Ronan's unexpected question jolted her out of her thoughts and into speech before she had time to consider further.

'I think you should buy this place.'

'Do you now?' Ronan returned cynically. 'Would that sudden conviction have anything to do with whatever Miss Gordon had to say? Oh, yes, I saw her hurry away from you just now. Aren't you afraid I'll take everything she's got and bleed her dry?'

The flare of anger in his eyes was matched by a dark smile that told her he was well aware of the quandary his sardonic question had forced on her, and he gave a low, grim laugh.

'I tell you what. You can sit in on the negotiations when I talk to her, and if you think I'm cheating her you only have to say. Oh, don't look so sceptical, darling! I promise you—anything you don't like comes out of the contract straight away.'

Lily's nerves knotted painfully at the thought of trying to confront him over anything—least of all when he was on his own territory, so to speak.

'But I don't know anything about...'

'You've run your own business for years, haven't you? You're no fool, Lily, you know what's fair and what's not. Just think of what you'd have wanted for Davey and take it from there.'

Think of what you'd have wanted for Davey. The message of those words seemed to reverberate round the room, picking up ominous echoes that warned her they had meant much more than just their surface interpretation.

'Ronan...?'

But he had already gone, shouldering his way across the room towards where Allie Gordon now stood behind the bar. Lily twisted her hands together in her lap. The thought of taking any part in the future of this girl and her family was awesome in its sense of responsibility.

But from the moment Ronan settled the girl at their table, buying her a drink before he launched into a concise summary of what he proposed, Lily knew she had nothing to fear. There wasn't a single thing in all he said that she could object to in any way. Unversed in the details of such business deals as she was, it all seemed perfectly fair—more than that, in fact.

'Well?' Ronan enquired when the negotiations were over and Allie, a wide, excited smile on her face, had left them alone again. 'Nothing to say? I never expected you to be so silent.'

'That's because I couldn't criticise a thing,' Lily admitted honestly. 'You've been more generous than I ever imagined.'

'It was no more than Davey got,' he told her, frowning darkly when she turned frankly sceptical golden eyes on him. 'Oh, for God's sake, Lily! Do you really believe that just because *this* kid's female, quite beautiful and shaped like a perfect Venus, I'd offer her a better deal than I gave your brother?'

'N-no.'

It wasn't at all comfortable to realise that the feelings that tied her tongue into knots weren't caused by his comments about her brother. She had to face the fact that the twisting pang of misery—of bitter *jealousy*—was caused by the fact that he'd said the other girl was beautiful and shapely.

She had liked him too. It had been written all over her face. In her radiant smile, the way she had looked deep into his face, the husky note in her voice. Lily had been shocked to find herself wanting to put a hand on Ronan's arm in a blatant 'hands off, he's mine' gesture of possession.

And just what would Ronan have thought of that? Of her laying claim to a marriage that didn't exist? A marriage she had denied earlier that evening by throwing the ring he had given her into the canal. And a marriage he had never intended to be real, seeing it only as the ultimate act of revenge.

Hastily she tried to change a subject that had become too uncomfortable to tolerate.

'You surprised me in another way this evening—in that club. I never saw you as a rock music fan.'

'I like *music*, full stop,' Ronan returned. 'Anything and everything.'

'So do you just listen, or do you perform as well? Do you play an instrument?'

'I wish I did, but it's a skill I've never acquired.'

Lily's head went back, her eyes widening and a smile curving the fullness of her lips.

'The great Ronan Guerin admitting to a failing! Now you *have* surprised me.'

'Good.' His eyes danced, picking up glints of gold from the lamps above them. 'I meant to. You have some major illusions about me that I'd like to disabuse you of.'

That caught her on the raw, with its echoes of the pointed

remark he had made about Davey only moments before, destroying the relaxed mood that had settled round them.

'Like the fact that you never loved me? Oh, don't worry! I certainly don't labour under *that* particular delusion any more. You *disabused* me on that score only too thoroughly.'

'Did I ever claim I loved you?' Ronan shot back, with a ferocity that made her reel backwards as if he had actually lifted a hand to slap her in the face.

Had he?

Eyes dark with shock, she looked back over the few short weeks of their courtship, the rush to their hasty marriage. 'I want you,' he had said. 'I have to have you. You must marry me!' But never a word of love.

And like a fool, head over heels in her own feelings, lost in her own dream of perfection and happy ever after, she had supplied those words for him, deceiving herself into believing that she had actually heard them.

'No...' she admitted slowly. 'No, you didn't.'

His nod was a gesture of dark satisfaction. Case for the prosecution proved. No room for argument.

'And now...'

But Lily couldn't take any more. Couldn't sit here and let him drive home even more just how little she had actually meant to him. How he had used her so callously for his own cruel ends. It would be like pounding blunt nails into an already raw and desolated heart.

Pushing back her chair with an ugly scraping sound, she got to her feet in a rush.

'I'm tired. I want to go home.'

But Belvedere House didn't feel like home any more. For the first time since Ronan had taken her there on their wedding day, the house seemed to have lost its warmth. It no longer had the sense of security that had made her feel so safe there. Now it was somehow cold and alien to her.

She couldn't forget that Ronan had bought it. Ronan had meant it to be yet another part of his hateful scheme. He had led her to believe that it was the home of her dreams when he'd

planned to destroy those dreams before they even had a chance
to form.

'Cold?' Ronan had caught her shiver of distress.

'A little. The rain's cooled the air.'

That was an approximate truth. The shower that had broken
during the journey home had brought a distinct chill with it, but
Lily knew that the feeling that gripped her was emotional rather
than physical.

'The room would soon warm up if I lit a fire.'

This time the shudder that shook her slim body in the rose-
coloured dress was more convulsive. She couldn't cope with that.
Not now; not ever while Ronan was nearby. Nightmare images
of heat and smoke filled her mind, pushing her close to panic.

'There's no need!'

'It won't take a moment...'

His persistence seemed to scrape at her already overstretched
nerves. Every other night he had let her end the evening whenever she chose, making no comment or protest when she gave
some excuse in order to retire early. But now he seemed intent
on keeping her here and prolonging the evening further.

'I said there's no need!' Distress made her voice sharp. 'I'm
tired. I'll be much warmer in bed.'

'Alone?'

'Of course alone!'

But even as she spoke her treacherous body tingled in a disturbing recollection of how it had felt *not* to lie alone in the wide
king-sized bed. How it had been when Ronan's long, powerful
body lay beside her, curved close against her spine. How it had
felt to have him move over her, cover her...

'Why are you so keen to get upstairs all of a sudden?'
Suspicion sharpened the question, narrowing the blue-grey eyes
as they swung round the room, as if searching for something. 'Is
Davey back? Have you seen...?'

'Davey? No!'

The quaver of her voice on the words was the result of a
sudden and stunning revelation that had suddenly slammed home
in her mind. At times tonight she had actually *forgotten* about
Davey, and Ronan's campaign of revenge. For just a few brief

moments she had wanted to be with Ronan as it had been before, when they had been together as a couple, just the two of them, with nothing else to interfere.

And he had felt the same. She *knew* he had. Often during the evening she had looked up to find his eyes, strangely darkened, fixed on her, and it had been there in the burning intensity of his gaze, an intensity he had never tried to hide.

She'd seen it, too, when they had danced together, and again when he had leant so close to her at the bar. Even when he had been angry with her that electric current of awareness had still sparked between them, holding them together with a magnetism that was too strong to be denied.

And perhaps she could use that feeling in order to help her brother. She should have used it that way before now, pressing home her advantage while she still had one.

'Ronan, please—about Davey.'

'I don't want to hear about your bloody brother!' Ronan snarled, but she forced herself to persist in spite of the ferocity of the glare he subjected her to, the seam of threat that ran through his words.

'But you must listen! *Why* won't you take back this house, or at least let me sell it and give you the money to pay what my brother owes? It's the very least—'

'And that would leave you without a home. You've given up your flat so where would you live?'

'I—I'd manage.'

Lily was only listening to the question with part of her mind. Most of her attention was centred on the way Ronan had reacted, on the faint, instinctive response he had made to her words 'what my brother owes'. That combined with the realisation that his concern for her well-being was genuine and unrestrained to leave her feeling strangely uncomfortable.

'I wouldn't hear of it.' It was flat, unyielding, no room for negotiation. 'And I don't want to discuss it any further. I want to forget all about Davey and his sins for tonight. I want to talk about us.'

'Like you said before. There isn't any "us".'

But even as she spoke she recognised the lie for what it was.

Nothing more than a defence, a fragile shield put up against the effect he was having on her mind and her heart. If Ronan could see how pitifully weak and inadequate it was, he could brush it aside with a single contemptuous flick of his hand.

Or the right words.

'There could be if you let it happen,' he said, the softness of his voice curling around her like warm, scented smoke so that she struggled to ignore the enticement in it. 'We're here together...'

'We're here by accident! Here in the house but in no way *together*. The reasons...'

She didn't dare mention Davey again. That was to risk destroying the tenuous peace that had formed between them.

'The reasons why you're here make that impossible.'

'But it doesn't make sense that we should both deny what we want.'

'Both...deny—I'm *not*!' She couldn't put into words what she feared he meant.

'You're lying to yourself again, my Lily.'

Ronan hadn't moved, hadn't taken a single step towards her, but all the same she felt his closeness like the static in the air before a violent thunderstorm. At any moment she expected to hear the crash of thunder, see the flare of lightning, and knew that her whole life was in danger of going up in flames in an instant.

'There's only that man we won't mention to come between us, and he's not here. So what's to stop us spending what's left of the rest of the night together?'

There's the fact that I love you and you feel nothing for me, she answered silently. The fact that anything you do will just be the result of uncaring lust, nothing more. An unemotional response to a very primal urge, a taking of pleasure as primitive and basic as any animal might indulge in.

And yet she would be lying to herself if she didn't admit that she was tempted.

She was supremely conscious of his height and breadth as he stood beside her. Every nerve seemed to be on red alert to the musky scent of his body, the burnished colour of his hair where it fell onto his forehead above those brilliant blue-grey eyes. It was impossible not to recall the exhilaration she had felt when they had danced together, the tiny electric shocks of awareness that had pricked at her spine when he had touched her.

She wanted this man as much as she had ever wanted him on her wedding day. More so, because then she had been innocent, unaware of the ecstasy of fulfilment his lovemaking could bring her. And nothing that had happened since then had changed a thing.

Plenty more fish in the sea. That had been Hannah's pragmatic response when she had heard of Ronan's desertion. But the simple fact was that she didn't *want* anyone else. She yearned to feel this man's arms enclose her, know the heated delight of his kisses on her skin. But above all else she wanted to make love with him. And she wanted it *now*.

What is to stop us spending what's left of the night together?

Drawing in a raw, uneven breath, she knew there was only one answer.

'Nothing.' She heard her voice say it before the thought had fully formed in her mind.

'Nothing?' Ronan echoed on a very different note.

Still he didn't move, and Lily was sure that he sensed, as she did, how precariously balanced the moment was. One false move and she would take flight, fleeing like some panic-stricken bird sighting a hungry cat, heading for the sanctuary of her room.

But each moment that she stayed the yearning, the need that had been barely under control all this time was growing stronger. Already it was gnawing at her deep inside, making her feel the slight distance between them—a couple of metres at most—as a vast, yawning chasm. So easy to cross and yet so totally impossible to bridge.

'Do you know what you're saying?'

Did she? She couldn't think, and anyway rationality had no part to play in all this. She was all sensitivity, all feeling, suffused with hunger. Wanting his touch, the power of his arms around her. Fearful of his possession and yet needing the profound intimacy of that moment as intensely as she needed to breathe, to feel her heart beat, the blood pulsing in her veins.

'I think perhaps I should just leave.'

He actually turned towards the door.

'No!'

It was wrenched from her, impossible to hold back.

Rationally she would have said that to have him leave was what she wanted most. But she had already accepted that rationality had nothing to do with what she was feeling. It was as if her mind was formed like an iceberg. The top part might be capable of logical, sensible thoughts, but underneath it was a huge, uncontrollable mass, made up of emotional drives and purely instinctive needs.

'No meaning, No, don't go? Or, No, my attentions are not wanted?'

'I...'

It was as if everything she was feeling had gathered in a knot at the top of her throat, threatening to choke her. She couldn't get any words past the blockage, but she had to speak. She didn't want him to know. She felt that she would die if he walked out of the door.

'I...'

In desperation she brought her hands up before her face in a frightened, defensive gesture.

'Lily...'

Striding forward, Ronan caught her hands in both of his, pulling them down with an ease that made a nonsense of her faint attempt at struggle. The face he revealed to his searching gaze was pale and strained, her golden eyes wide and brilliant.

'If it helps, I don't like feeling this way any more than you do,' he declared harshly. 'But there's nothing we can do about it. This force is there, Lily, whether we like it or not. It flashes between us whenever we're together, and it has the power of a storm, of a whirlwind that knocks us off our feet. It would be madness to deny it or try to contain it. That would only make it feed on itself and grow beyond all imagining.'

'I—know.'

Hadn't she tried to deny it to herself, only to find that with each breath she took it rooted deeper into her soul, the hunger growing by as much again with each second she spent in Ronan's company? But *her* need was fuelled by feeling, by the love she had for him. *His* need was the physical passion without emotion he had admitted to her earlier.

'But what can we do?'

'We can stop fighting it, my lovely Lily. Give in to what we're feeling, what we know is inevitable. We can indulge it, let it ravage us, and pray, pray like hell, that in time it will burn itself out.'

He moved closer, one arm sliding round her waist and drawing her close up against him so that she could feel the heated force of the desire that drove him, an untamed wildness hidden beneath the outwardly civilised clothing.

'We can do this...' Burning lips pressed against her cheek, sliding down the smooth curve of her jaw. 'And this...' His tongue tantalised the delicate skin of her ear lobe. 'Is this what you want?'

Her heart was thudding so violently that she could hear the sound of her own blood pounding like thunder in her ears. Her whole body was on fire, the flare of need building from a small flame to a raging inferno in the space of a heartbeat. The only response she could make was an inarticulate sound that might have been a cry of surrender.

'Let me show you...'

His mouth was perilously close to hers now, but still he held back the kiss she longed for, torturing her with his deliberate pause. Those deep indigo eyes watched her with calculating intensity as she moaned a hungry protest.

'Lily, I promised... I said a simple yes or no would suffice but I have to hear the word. I have to know what your answer is. You have to *tell* me—do you want this or...?'

But Lily could take no more. The inferno of need was raging out of control and she felt sure she would die if he didn't kiss her soon.

'Yes!' she breathed on a low, swooning sound. But then, suddenly afraid he hadn't heard, she repeated the word louder and with a desperate emphasis. '*Yes*. The answer's yes—oh, yes!'

CHAPTER TEN

THEY never made it up the stairs.

The need was too intense, the hunger out of control. Their mouths clashed, hands clung, bodies coiled around each other. It was more like a battle than actual lovemaking.

The need to be the first to touch the heated reality of skin, to press lips against its yielding warmth, drove them to tug at the restrictions of clothing, heedless of the dangers of ripping the material that stood in their way. Lily clawed at the buttons on his shirt, wrenching them from their fastenings with a ferocity that sent more than one spinning away into the shadows at the far corners of the room. Only when her fingers actually encountered the sleek muscles sheathed in the burning satin of his skin did her actions slow, a sigh of deepest contentment escaping her.

Ronan's teeth closed over one shoestring strap of her dress, tugging it down off her shoulder and exposing the fullness of the breast beneath.

'No bra.' It was a choked sound of satisfaction, one that echoed in the laughter deep in her throat.

'Under this?' she managed breathlessly, the question disintegrating into a moan of delight as his questing mouth found the poutingly erect nipple and closed over it, tugging softly.

'I knew I liked this dress.' Ronan's voice was thick and rough, his words muffled against her skin. 'I just didn't realise how much.'

The other strap was dealt with in the same way as the first, while, with his arms tight around her waist, Ronan manoeuvred her towards the settee, lowering her onto the green velvet cushions as he came down beside her.

Never once lifting his mouth from the path of tormenting pleasure he was inflicting on her, he shrugged himself free of the restriction of his shirt and tossed it aside, laughing exultantly as he heard her murmur of approval.

'This has to go.' Strong fingers made clumsy with need tugged at the silky hem of the rose-coloured dress. 'Much as I like it, it is definitely superfluous to requirements.'

A couple of swift tugs pulled it up and over her head, following his shirt to lie in a pool of material on the floor.

Lily was now nothing but a mass of quivering nerve-endings, her eyes half shut, her mouth open, her breath coming in ragged, uneven gasps. She grabbed at him with wild hands, holding him close so that the sensitised tips of her breasts rubbed against the soft abrasion of his body hair as she pressed greedy, demanding kisses on every part of his body she could reach. If she had wanted him, needed him before, it was as nothing to what she felt now.

That need made her bold, so that she fumbled with the leather belt around his narrow waist, sighing her contentment as she pulled it free of the buckle and moved on to the zip that fastened his trousers. With Ronan's willing assistance she soon dispensed with his remaining items of clothing, her fingers clawing their way down his exposed spine, feeling him arch and flex beneath her demanding touch.

'You asked for it, lady...' he muttered on a growl of very male hunger, pulling her beneath him and inserting one strong thigh between the silky smoothness of her legs.

But somehow he found the control to hold back just a second longer, so that she felt she might almost die of frustration if he didn't ease the burning need that centred deep in the most feminine heart of her body. She tilted her hips, curved her legs around him in an invitation as primitive and instinctive as womanhood itself, smiling to herself as she heard his groan of surrender.

With a muttered oath Ronan surged deep inside her with a speed and force that took her breath away, driving her almost over the edge in the space of a couple of fevered heartbeats. She cried his name on a sound of hot, primal pleasure, and then was lost, utterly abandoned to everything but the drive towards the ultimate fulfilment.

It was a long, long time before she came anywhere close to reality. But even when she surfaced from the heated waves of

delight that had flooded through her in the aftermath of a second
and then a third repeat of the ecstasies Ronan had driven her to,
she tried hard to cling to the haze of sensuality that clouded her
thoughts. She didn't want to face the fact that the volcano of
hunger that had erupted between them was all there was. That
there was no other feeling on which to build.

It didn't mean a thing, she told herself. One day, and probably
sooner rather than later, this idyll would be over and all she
would be left with was her memories. But right now she couldn't
bring herself to care. For now she had all she wanted, and she
would face the reality of the future when she had to. And until
that happened, for as long as she could, she would pretend that
all was right with her world.

Lily rolled over in bed, yawned, stretched luxuriously, then froze
into shocked immobility.

The reason for her consternation was twofold. Firstly there was
the space beside her. A space that on every other morning had
been filled by the warm, muscled bulk of Ronan's long-limbed
body but now was empty and smooth, already cool, with no trace
of the heat that usually lingered if he'd only just got up.

The second, more unexpected realisation was the fact that the
sun was blazing in through the curtains in a way that had her
reaching for her watch in near panic.

'Ten-thirty! But it can't be!'

She was still staring at it, trying to make some sense of what
she saw, when the door was pushed open sharply and Ronan
came into the room, a laden tray in his hands.

'Good morning, birthday girl. Breakfast is served.'

'Breakfast—but I can't. I—'

'Back into bed!'

Depositing the tray on the dressing table, Ronan restrained her
firmly when she flung back the quilt and would have swung her
legs to the ground.

'Ronan, I *can't*! Look at the time. I should have been in work
hours ago. I have to—'

Once more she broke off as he shook his dark head at her
worried urgency.

'You have to do nothing but sit back and enjoy yourself.' Still that firm hand on her shoulder held her when she tried to wriggle free. 'Hold still, woman! No one's expecting you at work. I rang and told them that you wouldn't be in.'

'You did what?'

Astonishment knocked all the fight out of her and she subsided back onto the pillows, staring up at him in blank bewilderment.

'But why?'

Even as she framed the question something registered in her mind. Something Ronan had said as he came through the door but she had been too anxious to notice. His next words confirmed that she *had* heard what she'd thought.

'Everyone should have a day off on their birthday,' he tossed over his shoulder as he turned back to pick up the tray again. 'And besides, I have plans for today that don't include sharing you with a bunch of florists—sorry about the pun.'

'Ouch!'

Lily managed an exaggerated grimace of amused disgust even as her heart clenched at that possessive 'I have plans...' But the next moment a degree of confusion was back again.

'How did you know it was my birthday?'

The tray was dumped on her lap with such force that she didn't have to look into Ronan's face in order to know his mood had changed for the worse.

'I *was* there when we applied for the marriage licence.' His voice was clipped and taut. 'We both had to give our dates of birth then.'

Of course. Lily sighed inwardly as her hands went out to steady the cup of coffee that had been rattled in its saucer by such rough treatment. She should have remembered. But, knowing that their marriage had meant so little to him, she had never expected that any part of it would have registered as being of any importance—least of all a minor detail like the date of her birthday.

This was how life with Ronan had been throughout the past week or so. One moment he was relaxed and approachable, seemingly at ease, the next he could switch to being icily distant and hostile. It was as if he was a weather vane that suddenly swung from one compass point to another in response to any change in the direction of the wind.

'Your cards.' Ronan tossed a bundle of brightly coloured envelopes onto the bed beside the tray. 'Nothing from Davey,' he added nastily as she gathered them up. 'I checked.'

And if there had been one he would most likely have noted the postmark and got straight on the phone to tell his private detective just where Davey had been when he'd sent it, Lily reflected miserably. It left a sour taste in her mouth to think that even today Ronan couldn't forget his private vendetta against her brother.

'We never made a big deal of birthdays in our family,' she said with a sigh. The truth was that her parents hadn't lived to see Davey reach his eleventh birthday, and after that there had been precious little money for presents or special treats.

'All the more reason for you to do so today. Everyone should have at least one day on which they feel really special. I remember that Rosalie used to say—'

Intent on opening one of the cards, Lily didn't notice his abrupt silence until it had dragged out to an unnerving length of time. Then, disturbed by the sudden tension that seemed to close around her, she lifted her head and frowned enquiringly.

'Rosalie?' she questioned, worried by the way those changeable eyes had no warmth in them but were the bleak, threatening grey of the North Sea on a winter's day.

'Someone I—knew.' His voice was as ravaged as his eyes.

'Someone special?'

He had cared for her; that much was obvious. The way he had spoken her name had left her in no doubt of that.

'Very special,' Ronan confirmed curtly.

He had no intention of expanding on his minimal response, it was clear, and Lily didn't dare to press him.

This Rosalie was probably some ex-girlfriend, she decided. That would explain his reluctance to talk about her. The thought that he might actually have *loved* the unknown woman, in a way he had never cared for her, brought a rush of burning tears to her eyes so that she had to blink hard to drive them away.

'Eat your breakfast before it gets cold.'

Lily struggled to obey Ronan's instruction, but the food stuck in her throat, impossible to swallow.

What had happened between Ronan and this Rosalie? Had she ended their relationship, because it seemed that he still had some strong feelings for her? Or...

The disturbing thought slammed home so hard that she actually caught her breath in shock. Had this Rosalie, too, been sacrificed to the black hatred of Davey that drove Ronan? Could he have put the other girl aside to marry Lily herself? Was it possible that once their travesty of a marriage had served its purpose he would cut himself free and go back to his former love?

'You've been staring at that card for more than a minute.' Ronan's voice broke into her thoughts, making her start like a nervous cat.

'I—was reading the verse,' she managed, knowing full well from the look of contempt that he turned on the four lines of doggerel she held up that he was not convinced by her explanation. Needing to distract herself, she reached for the next one.

It was from Ronan himself, she realised, recognising the forceful confidence of the writing. That thought made her fingers unsteady, the rapid beat of her heart impossible to control as she opened the envelope.

For a couple of seconds her eyes blurred, making it impossible to focus on the picture on the card. But at last they cleared and she recognised a copy of a painting she had said she loved.

'It's beautiful—thank you.'

What had you expected, stupid? she berated herself. That he would have bought some elaborately romantic card—'For my darling wife with all my love'? Whatever else he was, Ronan was not such a hypocrite as to be party to a lie like that. But she had to admit that just for a moment she had hoped, allowed herself to dream.

'So, what would you like to do today?'

'I thought you had plans.'

'They're mainly for this evening. I thought you'd like to choose how to spend your time before then.'

'Could we go out? Onto the moors, perhaps?'

'Whatever you like.' Ronan eased his long body off the bed, collecting the discarded envelopes from her cards as he went.

'Why don't you think about it while you're dressing and let me know what you've decided? Today, your wish is my command.'

If only she could believe that, Lily reflected as the door swung to behind him. If only she could truly tell Ronan what was on her mind and in her heart, as she might have done if that uncomfortable distance hadn't come between them with the mention of Rosalie's name and if she had been able to speak openly.

The thought of just how he might have reacted if she'd told him that what she wanted most was for him to strip off the denim shirt and jeans he was wearing and join her in the bed made her shift uneasily under covers that had suddenly become uncomfortably warm. What she had needed was for him to slide in beside her, draw her to him and make wild, passionate love to her until she was unable to think about this Rosalie, or Davey, or anything. Until she was reduced to such a state of pure feeling that nothing else mattered but Ronan and herself and the powerful force they had created between them.

Showered and dressed, in a green floral top and skirt, she was on her way downstairs when the phone rang in the hall. Taking the last couple of steps in a single jump, she reached it in seconds, snatching it up just as Ronan appeared in the doorway opposite.

'Hello?'

Her heart missed several beats as an all too familiar voice spoke her name.

'Oh, Dav—'

Frantically she swallowed down the rest of the name that would have revealed the identity of her caller to the dark, watchful observer at the other side of the hall.

'Daisy,' she amended carefully. 'How lovely to hear from you.'

'Daisy?' her brother echoed in obvious confusion. 'Lill, what the hell...?'

'It's Daisy Marchant, *Ronan*.' Lily deliberately emphasised the last name. 'An old friend from school.'

'He's still there, then?' The despair in Davey's voice tore at her heart. 'Is that what you're trying to tell me?'

'That's right!' she improvised, with what she hoped was airy gaiety. 'It must have been last year! I— *No!*'

Her sentence ended on a cry of shock and horror as the receiver was snatched from her hand. Some look, gesture, or intonation must have given her away. Ronan, clearly not deceived at all, was now glaring at the instrument as if he believed it was Davey himself, his hand clenched as tightly as he obviously wished he could fasten it around the younger man's throat.

'Ronan—don't!'

Ronan wished he could wring Davey's neck. The little wretch had to know that today was Lily's birthday, so would it be too much to ask that he consider her feelings for once, instead of his own? Her sudden pallor when she had heard his voice, the unshed tears that were making her honey-coloured eyes unnaturally brilliant were all eloquent testimony to the distress she felt. She didn't deserve a brother like Davey, and he—in a very different way—didn't deserve to have a sister like her.

Ronan's breath hissed in between clenched teeth as he fought to control his instinctive response of blind fury. The way Lily looked twisted something savagely in his guts, with a reminder of the way that he, too, had once felt about Davey Cornwell. He had been full of admiration and, yes, affection for the little so and so. He had actually liked him a lot and had been determined to pull out all the stops for him, only to have it flung right back in his face.

But was it possible that there was some sort of explanation for what had happened? If the little fool would just come home, then perhaps they could do something about sorting out this hellish situation once and for all. He should tell him...

But then he looked into Lily's face again, and what he saw there drove away every reasonable thought.

'Cornwell!'

His tone sent shivers down Lily's spine. She could just imagine how Davey must feel, hearing it when he was somewhere completely alone and feeling lost already. 'Where the hell are—? Hell and damnation, he's gone!'

'And what else did you expect?'

Tension stretched Lily's voice tight as a guitar string. Her legs felt unsteady beneath her and she flung out a hand to clasp the wooden banisters in order to support herself.

'Anyone would have done the same if they were subjected to an attack like that! What's the matter, Ronan?' she went on as he slammed the receiver back into its cradle, a dark scowl twisting his face. 'Did your prey get away from you again?'

Prey was right, she thought nervously, seeing the ferocious glare he turned on her. Right now Ronan looked like nothing so much as some hungry tiger, unexpectedly thwarted of a kill he had anticipated with cruel confidence.

'Were you hoping to keep him talking until your hired thugs could track him down? Have you put a tracer on my phone or are you having all my calls tapped?'

'Don't be stupid!' Ronan snapped. 'I'm doing no such thing.'

'No? Well, I wouldn't put it past you! Where Davey's concerned you're so eaten up with hate you can't see straight. Well, you know what they say about revenge, don't you? That it has a nasty habit of going sour on you. That it can turn round and bite you when you least expect it.'

'Tell me about it,' Ronan drawled, in a voice dark with undertones she couldn't begin to interpret.

'Going sour' just about summed it up, he reflected. What had happened to the strength of purpose, the conviction that he was right which had driven him from the start? He seemed to have lost it somewhere along the way, and with that loss had come the uncomfortable feeling that perhaps things had not been quite as black and white as he had believed. And that was a thought that didn't make for a comfortable conscience or an easy relationship with Lily.

'So, seeing as you've decided to number me amongst the devil's spawn, at least as far as your precious brother is concerned, does that mean today's trip is off?'

'You couldn't be more right!'

It was only when she heard the words spoken aloud that Lily was forced to reconsider. Was he really as much the villain in all this as Davey had led her to believe? Reluctantly she recalled that night in the wine bar, when she had commented on the terms of the offer he had made to Allie Gordon.

'It was no more than Davey got,' he had said. But at the time she hadn't taken him up on that point, and since then the sheer physical intensity of their relationship had driven all other thoughts from her mind. Now she was forced to think about it, and to wonder.

'You never did buy that other place,' she said slowly.

Ronan frowned his confusion at her abrupt change of subject, but a couple of seconds later he realised just what she was talking about.

'The club? No. It was OK, I suppose, but nothing really special.'

She was getting better at reading his face now. She knew him well enough to realise that behind the almost throwaway comment lurked other things he hadn't said. Things he didn't want to say.

'And was Davey special?'

Ronan's eyes were clouded and stormy, revealing more than he wanted to, she was sure of that.

'Davey was special,' he confirmed sombrely.

'Tell me...'

'Not now!' It was an angry snarl. 'You may want to ruin your birthday by dragging your brother into the conversation at every turn, but quite frankly I am sick of the sound of his name. Today was supposed to be for you, but you've made it clear you don't want any of it. You'd rather die than go out anywhere with me— so I take it you won't want this either?'

It was only when he lifted his left hand that Lily realised how all this time he had been holding a small square package wrapped in beautiful silver paper.

'What's that?' It was impossible to suppress her curiosity, and one corner of Ronan's mouth curled up in response to the unguarded question.

'A birthday present.'

'For me?'

'Of course for you. That is what usually happens on birthdays.

Family and friends—even husbands sometimes—buy gifts for the person whose birthday it is.'

He held it out towards her, temptingly just out of reach. Those indigo eyes were fixed on her face, that expressive mouth twisting slightly as he watched the conflict between natural curiosity and wary suspicion move across it.

'But if you think it would be like selling your soul to accept it, then...'

To her shock and consternation he moved abruptly, dropping the parcel into a nearby wastepaper bin where it fell with an ominous thud.

'Ronan!' The protest came automatically. 'You can't do that!'

The shrug of his broad shoulders dismissed her objection carelessly.

'I just have done. I bought it for you, but if you don't want it...'

'Oh, but I do!'

The words were out before she had time to consider if they were wise. The thought that he had gone out and chosen something just for her, something so personal that he was fully prepared to throw it away if she didn't want it, meant so much. She didn't know just what it signified on Ronan's part, but it had to mean *something*.

'I should have known no woman could resist a present.'

Lily had to struggle to ignore the sardonic bite of the comment as she retrieved the parcel from the bin into which he had so ignominiously dumped it. But she looked up quickly enough to catch the amused smile that he hadn't been able to suppress as he watched her.

Suddenly it occurred to her that she had been skilfully outmanoeuvred, carefully distracted from the matter in hand, so that he didn't have to answer awkward questions. But for the sake of peace she decided it was better to leave things as they were. Perhaps they could enjoy today after all. There would be all the time in the world to talk tomorrow.

And so she pushed all her worries to the back of her mind as she ripped the wrapping paper off the parcel she held.

'Oh, Ronan!'

She had expected perfume, perhaps, or jewellery. The sort of present men turned to when they had no idea what else to buy for the women in their lives. But what she saw was an old leather-bound book on gardening, filled with the most beautiful hand-coloured prints of all the flowers. It was the sort of thing she would have bought for herself if she had been able to afford it—which was unlikely, because it was obvious that it was a first edition and so very costly indeed.

'It's wonderful! Gorgeous!'

Her voice cracked slightly on the word. The book must have taken some tracking down, and it was much more carefully chosen than she had ever expected.

'I don't know how to thank you.'

Which was nothing more than the truth. The impulse to throw herself into his arms, press an ardent kiss onto the lean plane of his cheek was almost overwhelming, but she forced herself to resist it. Ronan would not welcome it, and she didn't think she could cope with any display of obvious lack of enthusiasm, the withdrawal she felt sure would follow.

'I can think of a way.'

Some of Lily's delight evaporated and she eyed Ronan warily, meeting his dark blue gaze with more than a little suspicion.

'Oh, Lily, you are so transparent!' Ronan laughed. 'Is that the only thing you can think I'd want from you? There are other things in life.'

'Such as?' Lily demanded gruffly. There might be other things in life, but sex was all he ever seemed to want from her.

'Let's call a truce,' Ronan said, taking the wind out of her sails completely. 'Just for today let's forget about your brother, pretend he never existed. Let's forget *everything* and let it be as it was the first time we met.'

But then he had sought her out deliberately. He had already had his cruel plan of revenge fully formed in his head, while she had been innocent, naïve and easy prey to his predatory, cynical seduction.

But, oh, she wanted that truce he offered! Wanted it so much that the need was like a bruise in her heart, aching unbearably. Just for a day, he had said, and the thought of twenty-four hours of peace with him was the best birthday present she could imagine.

'Lily?' Ronan prompted when she couldn't answer, and the intensity with which he used her name shocked her into speech.

'All right,' she said jerkily. 'I think I can manage that.'

In the end it was surprisingly easy. Having declared a truce, Ronan went out of his way to be as charming and attentive as only he knew how. The day sped past, their trip out a delight, and in the evening, after she had changed into a bronze velvet shift that mirrored the colour of her eyes, Ronan took her out to dinner.

And that was when the only small flaw in Lily's enjoyment forced her to recall that things were not quite as perfect as they seemed. Because the restaurant Ronan had chosen was, for obvious reasons, not the one that was their absolute favourite in the area. He couldn't take her there and still hold to the terms of their truce because it had been there, just three weeks after he had met her, that he had asked her to marry him.

But with Ronan in his present mood it was possible to pretend that even that had never happened. The delicious food and wine helped too, and by the end of the evening Lily was able to turn to him and say, with genuine honesty, 'I've had a wonderful birthday, Ronan, the best in years! Thank you so much. I really did enjoy everything...'

He wasn't listening, his attention apparently drawn to something unseen behind her back. There was a strange, secretive smile on his lips, and those steely eyes seemed to gleam in what she could only describe as anticipation.

'Ronan? What...?'

Some faint sound, a flurry of activity, made her curious. She half turned her head, saw the cake in a waitress's hands, then froze in horror.

Flames. Dancing golden flames dazzling her eyes, so close to her that she could feel their heat on her skin. She could hear the faint hiss and crackle as they burned, catch the smell of the drifting smoke.

'*No!*'

Panic closed her throat, her heart racing painfully, pounding the blood through her veins until her head swam sickeningly.

'Happy birthday, Lily.'

Through the spinning haze she heard Ronan's voice, blurred and distorted. There was no way that she could move or respond. Even worse, there was no way she could communicate her fear.

'Lily?'

Her eyes were fixed wide, staring in terror. Her whole body was stiff with fear and rejection, one hand covering the mouth that was open in a silent scream.

Fire. Inside her head the delicate glow of the candles was transformed into a raging inferno, a white-hot blaze that raged through everything, burning up all she had ever held dear. Shattering, destroying, killing.

'No!'

She heard the high-pitched cry with a strange objectivity, only realising it was her own voice, tight with panic, after a couple of confused seconds.

'No! No! Oh, God, no!'

'Take it away!'

Another voice, cool and incisively authoritative, cut through the maelstrom of fear inside her head as Ronan leapt to his feet, one strong hand going out to push the waitress aside.

'Take the bloody thing out of here—now!'

A tall, powerful form came between her and those dreadful flames, the bulk of his chest and shoulders blocking out the sight of them, that terrible, flickering light. She was gathered up into strong, comforting arms, lifted from her chair and held tight against the heat of his body, her head against his chest where his heart raced almost as frantically as her own.

'Lily, sweetheart, it's all right. You're safe—quite safe.'

Safe. The word seemed to reverberate round and round inside Lily's skull in a disturbing echo of her own scream of panic.

Safe! The bitter irony of it broke through the icy grip of fear. It had her collapsing against Ronan's strength, weak, desolate tears escaping from the corners of her eyes and spilling out onto the immaculate white cotton of his shirt.

Because even through the panic, the horror and the pain of the memories that the sight of the flames had revived in her thoughts, one other sensation stood out clearly—one that devastated her totally.

In the moment that Ronan had taken her in his arms she had known such a rush of pleasure and joy, such a glorious sense of security that it was like coming home at last after a long and terrible journey. If she hadn't known before just how much she loved this man then she would have known it in that moment. Known that he had taken her heart and now held it captive so that her happiness, her future, her whole being was bound up with him for the rest of her life.

But the bitter truth was that her sense of security was built on a foundation so false, so rotten, that one unwary move would bring the whole edifice of their relationship crashing to the ground. Ronan felt nothing for her except the sexual passion he had demonstrated so clearly. He was perfectly capable of using her for his own satisfaction and then calmly walking away without a second thought. He had done it once already, and she knew he was quite prepared to do it again.

And, knowing that, Lily also had to face the way that her love for Ronan had exposed her to an even greater threat than the one posed by the flames. The emotional danger she was in was far, far worse than any physical hazard, and because of that, where Ronan was concerned, she would never, ever be safe again.

CHAPTER ELEVEN

'DO YOU feel ready to talk about it?'

It was perhaps an hour and a half since the sight of the candles on her birthday cake had flung her into a black pit of fear, one from which she had only managed to climb with great difficulty. During that time she had only been able to cling to Ronan, who had been a rock of strength and support to her.

He had half supported, half carried her from the restaurant, flinging a bundle of notes down on the table in payment for their half-completed meal, and taken her straight out to his car. He had driven home in a tight-lipped withdrawn silence, not speaking until she was installed on the settee in the sitting room and he had poured a large glass of brandy.

'Drink this,' he said gruffly, pushing the glass into her hand.

'I don't like brandy,' Lily protested, earning herself an exasperated roll of his eyes.

'Drink it!' The command was too forceful to risk the consequences of disobeying.

As she sipped cautiously he poured himself his own drink— almost the same size as her own, she noticed—and flung himself down in the chair opposite, long legs sprawled out in front of him. But after only one swallow of the fiery spirit he abandoned his drink and sat up straight again, folding his hands together and resting his chin on them as he regarded her with a brooding intensity that made her shift uneasily in her seat.

'Are you going to tell me about it?' he asked at last.

'What do you want to know?'

'Everything. Every damn thing! Like why you acted as if the end of the world had come just because...'

The cutting edge to his voice concealed the way he had actually felt at that moment. He couldn't describe what it had done to him to see her go to pieces like that, to see the fear and distress in her eyes and know that, however innocently, he was responsible. He had wanted to gather her up into his arms and never let her go. To tell her that he would keep her safe from everything from now until eternity. That she would have nothing to fear ever again.

But that sort of promise could only come from someone who loved her and whom she loved in return. He didn't know what he felt right now, but he was deadly clear on how Lily regarded *him*. She would never accept such a promise from him; in fact she was far more likely to run a million miles in the opposite direction. A blazing sex-life like theirs was no foundation for long-term trust. He had forfeited the right to that when he had married her out of revenge, wanting only to hurt.

'Just because of a few candles?' Lily set her glass down on a nearby table with such force that she was frankly surprised to see that it didn't shatter into a thousand pieces.

'*Just because* those candles reminded me of the worst day of my life. The day when my whole life went up in flames, when I lost almost everything I ever cared about. The day my parents burned to death in their own home!'

He hadn't expected that. His shock showed in the way his dark head went back, those stormy eyes widening as if she had actually reached out and slapped him hard in the face.

'What happened?' he asked, his voice sounding rough round the edges. 'Do you feel ready to talk about it?'

His obviously uncomfortable reiteration of his original question told Lily how he was feeling without words needing to be spoken. The unexpected sight of Ronan, arrogant, successful, confident Ronan Guerin, actually at a loss for the right thing to say gave her an unexpected boost in a way that the potent effect of the brandy could never have equalled.

Pulling herself upright, she smoothed back the tangled strands of her disordered blonde hair, wiped nervous hands along the skirt of her dress, searching for the best way to begin.

'It was just after Christmas—between then and the New Year. We still had the decorations up because we never took them down until Twelfth Night. Perhaps if we had...'

Her voice trailed away again as she struggled with her memories. Ronan waited in silence until she cleared her throat, ready to begin again.

'In the living room we had an old-fashioned open fire, one of those with a wooden mantelpiece over the top. Mum used to like to decorate it with candles and little figures all set into cotton wool, so that it looked like a snow scene—you know what I mean?'

She glanced up at Ronan to check that he understood and found herself transfixed by the blaze of that unmoving, fiercely intent scrutiny. His concentration on her was so complete, so absorbed that it took the space of a couple of heartbeats before he inclined his head in silent acknowledgement.

'Davey was only young, and he was fascinated by the candles. If we weren't careful he would try to light them himself, either with matches, or once he used a small piece of paper that he stuck in the fire...'

Dark memories were beating against her thoughts like powerful wings, and she had to swallow hard to ease the constriction in her throat. Ronan clearly noted her distress, and the way her fingers clenched over each other, but he did nothing, waiting in that rigid silence until she regained enough control to go on.

'On New Year's Eve we all stayed up to see the New Year in, and so we went to bed exhausted. I was sure that the fire had died down, that it was safe. Dad was usually so careful. He always put a guard up before he went upstairs. But that night some spark must have jumped onto a curtain, or perhaps a decoration fell. We'll never know.'

Unable to continue, she shook her head despairingly, dashing the back of her hand against her eyes to brush away the bitter tears.

'The whole house went up. The first I knew of it was when my dad banged on the bedroom door, yelling at me to wake up. By that time the lounge was alight, and the smoke...'

Her eyes darkened as she recalled the acidic, stinging sensation, the burning in her lungs that had made it so difficult to breathe.

'Dad got Davey and I up and out of the bedroom window, but Mum had stayed to look for something—I've no idea what. He went back to fetch her and I never saw either of them again. There was a terrible crash. I learned later that the stairs had given way and Mum and Dad were trapped upstairs. They both died.'

Ronan moved abruptly, but only to reach for his glass. He drained what was left in it in one long swallow. It was either that or give in to his urge to go to her, hold her tight. But she wouldn't welcome any such gesture, and right now she had enough to handle without the added pressure of anything he might do.

'I didn't know...' His voice was low, sounding rusty, as if it had come from a painfully dry throat. 'You were how old?'

'Seventeen.'

'Little more than a child. And Davey?'

'He was almost eleven. His birthday was the day after we buried our parents.'

The words themselves were hard enough, but what made it so much worse was the way that Ronan continued to hold himself aloof, the distance, both mental and physical, he deliberately put between them. He didn't move from his chair, made no gesture of concern or attempt to hold her and comfort her.

And she did so want to be held. She needed to know the solace of those strong arms around her, to feel someone cared.

But of course that was what was wrong. The truth hit her like a further cruel blow to an already wounded heart. Ronan didn't care. She had let the past days, with their form of peace, the new-found ease with which the two of them had been able to live together, lull her into a false sense of security. They hadn't been living or doing anything *together*. They had simply been existing in the same house.

Except for the sex, of course. And that was all it had ever been—pure sex, nothing more. Though there had been nothing remotely *pure* about it. On Ronan's part, at least, it had been just the passion without emotion that he had declared he wanted.

Lily felt suddenly totally, bone-numbingly weary, the adrenaline rush supplied by her earlier panic leaving her abruptly. She collapsed back against the cushions, as limp as a punctured balloon from which all the air had escaped.

'What happened to you both?'

'We were put into temporary accommodation—bed and break-fast. Davey hated it. He never adjusted to living with so many people, and he was bullied by some of the older boys.'

'Is that why you're so over-protective of him?'

A small flame of defiance flared in the shadowed amber of her eyes.

'I am not *over*-protective! Davey was so much younger than I was, and I felt responsible for him! He was scared and lost and he missed our parents desperately. As soon as I could, I got myself a job and a flat and Davey came with me.'

'And who looked after *you*?'

It was the last question she had expected. Looking sharply into Ronan's watchful eyes, Lily was surprised to see how pale and drawn he looked. He seemed to have lost all colour, and his skin appeared to be stretched tight over the forceful lines of his cheek-bones until it was almost transparent. Those clasped hands were clenched so tight that the knuckles showed white.

'I was older, and besides I didn't have to live with the dreadful fear that haunted my brother.'

The blue-grey eyes narrowed sharply. If his gaze had been fixed before, now it impaled her with all the force of a powerful laser.

'What fear?'

'He thought he was responsible for the fire that killed Mum and Dad. He admitted to me that he'd not been able to sleep and he'd gone downstairs. He hadn't been able to resist lighting the candles even though he'd been forbidden to do so. He thought he'd blown them out before he went back to bed but he couldn't be absolutely sure.'

There, it was out now. For the first time ever she'd revealed the dreadful fear that her brother had confided to her all those years ago. This was the shadow Davey carried with him every day, the cause of those black dreams that destroyed his peace at night.

'Poor Davey.' Ronan sounded surprised to find himself feeling sorry for him. 'This is what gives him the nightmares?'

Too astonished by his perceptiveness to speak, Lily could only nod numbly, unshed tears swimming in her brilliant golden eyes.

With a faint shudder she folded her arms around her slender body, as if to provide for herself the physical comfort she needed from him.

'He—he dreams of the fire.' A single tear welled up at the corner of one eye and she simply let it fall, too miserable, too drained to do anything more. 'So do I sometimes. When things get on top of me I...'

'Oh, hell—Lily!'

At last Ronan moved. In a swift, lithe movement he was up out of his chair and had caught her in his arms, pulling her close against the warm strength of his chest. His action shattered the last thread of her self-control so that, abandoning all attempt at restraint, she collapsed against him, her hands clutching at his shirt as she sobbed helplessly.

Ronan simply held her. She felt the power of his arms around her, heard his voice whispering words of comfort, soothing her until the violent storm had passed and she'd regained some degree of calm, her sobs subsiding to uneven, choking gasps. It was then that she twisted in his arms, lifting her face to his in the instinctive, unthinking gesture of a wounded child seeking comfort.

His hesitation was not what she'd expected. But it lasted only a second or two, and then Ronan was kissing her as she had wanted, his soft, featherlight caresses wiping away the lingering traces of her tears. His touch stabbed at her heart with such a bittersweet gentleness that aroused a soft, sensual longing deep inside, yet she knew that the comfort he offered her was basically flawed.

It was not the deep, committed care of someone who loved her and would do anything to help ease the pain deep inside. It was only the gesture of a man, any man, who could not just sit and watch her weep and do nothing.

But for now she would settle for that imperfect sort of giving. She was so desperate for the consolation of another human being, needing so desperately to be held, that she would give herself up to it without a second thought. She would let the physical passion that he could arouse so easily wipe her mind clean of every other unhappy thought.

In Ronan's arms she couldn't think of anything but him and the cyclone of hunger that whirled deep inside her, and right now all she wanted to do was to abandon herself to that mindless delight in order to be able to forget about everything else.

So it was the most devastating shock of all when Ronan swore savagely and wrenched himself away from her. The force of his movement took him halfway across the room to stand, hands pushed deep into his pockets, staring out of the window into the darkness of the night. At last he sighed and raked one hand roughly through his hair.

'We need to talk, Lily,' he said unevenly.

Talk. It was the last thing she wanted. But, even as she formed the fullness of her mouth into a moue of petulant protest, she was thoroughly taken aback to find that the gesture transformed itself into a wide, aching yawn. Without the warm support of Ronan's arms around her she felt exhausted, the emotions of the night having drained all her strength. Weakly she fell back against the arm of the settee, unable to hold back another yawn.

'But not tonight,' Ronan continued more quietly. 'You're worn out. You should be in bed.'

With you? Lily wanted to ask, but didn't dare. There was something new and very worrying in Ronan's mood. Something that put a distance between them she didn't know how to bridge. She could almost see the barriers, and signs spelling out only too clearly: Keep Out! No Entry!

So now she submitted silently to the cool, impersonal touch of his hands as he helped her from the settee. She let him support her up the stairs and into her bedroom.

Her bedroom, she noted, and not the room he slept in, where they had shared a bed and made love so gloriously and so passionately for the past week.

If anything spoke most clearly of the change in him, then it was this. Every other day he had kept clear of her bedroom, never coming into it, never even opening the door. But now he led her straight into it, lowering her to sit on the side of the bed.

'You'll need to sleep.'

He was halfway to the door again when it dawned on her that he really meant it. He actually planned to leave her alone. But she couldn't find the words to call him back. Her heart leapt in weak relief when he hesitated, seemed to relent, and swung back abruptly.

'Will you be able to rest?' he asked. 'What about those nightmares.'

Right now, he looked like the one who was haunted by dark demons, his eyes clouded and dull, lines of strain etched around his nose and mouth.

'There's one sure way of keeping them at bay.'

Lily patted the opposite side of the bed, lifting the quilt invitingly. When he didn't respond she tried a faint smile, her stomach quailing when it wasn't returned but was met with a coldly quelling glare.

'No.' It was as hard and unyielding as his stony expression.

'Ronan, please!'

If he left her like this she knew what the night would be like for her, the horrors that would haunt what little sleep she might have, and she couldn't bear it.

'No!' If possible it was even more emphatic than before, in spite of the fact that he hadn't raised his voice from a conversational level.

'But, Ronan, I'm scared! I'm afraid to be on my own. I'll never sleep...'

His sigh was a masterpiece of controlled resignation as once more he raked a rough hand through the darkness of his hair.

'You won't be on your own. I'll sleep here.'

A wave of his hand indicated the old-fashioned *chaise longue* that stood in the wide bay of the window.

'But you'll be desperately uncomfortable.'

'I'll manage.' He dismissed her concern with an indifference that stung bitterly.

'Ronan...'

'*No!* That's how it's to be, Lily. That or nothing. I spend the night here or I leave and you sleep entirely alone. What's it to be?'

She had no alternative but to agree. It was either that or face the terrors of the night alone. She had done that many times in the past, but somehow this time the prospect seemed so much worse.

And she knew why. Those nights spent wrapped in the comforting strength of Ronan's arms had brought home to her what real peace, real, relaxed sleep actually meant, and the thought of having to return to facing her nightmares on her own was more than she could bear. If she couldn't have Ronan's warm, strong body next to hers then she'd settle for his distant but nevertheless comforting presence. It was better than nothing at all.

In the end she slept surprisingly well, the strains of the night taking their toll. At first she knew a sense of restlessness, a yearning ache that suffused her body at the thought that Ronan was so near and yet so very far away, and she feared it might keep her awake all night. But that gave way to exhaustion, and once asleep she didn't wake until late the next morning when the sound of rain against the windowpane brought her awake at last.

Ronan was still there, his long body curled uncomfortably on the *chaise longue*. He was deeply asleep, his burnished hair falling in soft disarray across his face, long lashes lying like black crescents above his strong cheekbones. The blanket he had pulled over himself had fallen to the floor, tangled in a way that seemed to indicate a far more restless night than she had spent, revealing the navy pyjama trousers he had insisted on changing into before settling down for the night.

What had brought on such an uncharacteristic attack of modesty? Lily wondered, a sudden wave of uneasy vulnerability driving her to pull on the mint-green robe before sliding out of bed and padding across the room on bare feet to perch on the side of the old-fashioned settee. When they had shared a bed he had scorned the idea of any nightwear and had slept gloriously naked, his powerful body entwined with hers. So what had been so very different about last night?

As her mind fretted at the question Ronan stirred slightly and muttered in his sleep. As if sensing her gaze on him, he tensed suddenly. The next moment his blue-grey eyes flew open to meet her watchful golden gaze.

Ronan's first response was a warmly sensual delight that heated his blood, making him want to stretch indolently like a lazy cat lying basking in the sun. The soft weight of her body against his legs, the brush of her golden hair against the bare flesh of his chest and the scent of her skin, still flushed with sleep, were such a heady pleasure that every one of his senses swam in voluptuous delight, making him feel as if he was adrift on a warm, glowing tide.

But then she shifted slightly, the movement tugging the sides of her robe apart and exposing the velvet slopes of her breasts in the same second that his body came fully awake. The instant, clawing hunger was like a hot knife searing a path through every nerve, making him want to reach for her, pull her down beside him, wrench open the flimsy silk that was all that came between them...

Recollection of the events of the previous night was like a slap in the face from brutal, icy fingers, the feeling of guilty unease that followed strong enough to crush down even the most erotic of temptation. He had lain awake for hours after Lily had finally fallen asleep, going over and over things but always coming to the one, irrefutable conclusion.

There was no future for him and Lily unless he was completely straight with her and told her everything. The trouble was that deep down inside he feared the effect that truth would have once it was revealed.

The possibility that there was no future for the two of them, no matter what, was what had kept him awake in the early hours of the morning. And the real complication was that he had just come to realise how much he *wanted* that future, only to face the possibility of having it snatched away from him.

But first they had to talk. And so he schooled his expression into one of a calm control he was light-years away from feeling and even managed a faint smile.

'Good morning.'

It had taken only a couple of seconds, but Lily had seen the swift, careful adjustment of his expression, the switch from sleepy sensuality, to slightly unfocused wariness, and then to an apparently relaxed control. And it was that control that worried her. It seemed that whatever had kept him distant from her last night still clouded his thoughts this morning.

'Did you sleep OK?'

'I was fine.'

Lily's response was uneven, raw-edged. She sensed that, like her, he was thinking back to the first day of their marriage, when she had woken to find him looking down at her much as she was doing to him now.

'How about you?'

He looked dreadful. As if the few seconds' sleep that she had witnessed since she'd woken had been all the rest he'd actually managed. Her concern grew as he stretched slowly, grimacing in discomfort as he tested muscles that had obviously stiffened into their cramped positions.

'I'll live.'

It was a throwaway line, one that didn't ring quite true in its casual nonchalance. But Lily didn't have time to consider what lay behind it before he spoke again.

'Lily, about last night. I want you to know that I knew nothing of this. Davey never said a word about your parents and how they died. If I'd known what you'd been through, I'd never have—'

'Never have married me?' Lily jumped in far too quickly.

She wished he hadn't stirred. The movement of sitting up had brought into play muscles that she knew from experience had a whipcord strength when they folded round her body. Watching them slide and bunch under the smooth skin, lightly covered in dark hair, dried her mouth and made her heart flutter uncomfortably.

'No.' It was a flat, unemotional declaration. 'I would never have married you. I'm only sorry that I did.'

Did he know how much it pained her to hear him say that? Lily's hand went to her mouth to hold back the whimper of distress that almost escaped her. Perversely, the fact that he was apologising for having gone through their pantomime marriage ceremony now seemed to hurt more than discovering the truth about that event ever had.

'You can't know how much I regret that.'

Feeling as if some red-hot knife was hacking out her heart with brutal, clumsy cuts, Lily had to drag up from the depths of her soul the courage to retort, 'But you wanted revenge—someone to repay Davey's debts.'

'*Debts!*' Ronan echoed with black cynicism, swinging his long legs off the chaise and getting to his feet, pacing about the room as if he couldn't bear to be still a moment longer. 'No one can replace what your brother took from me!'

Lily took a deep, steadying breath. She'd said it once and she'd say it again and again until he believed her.

'I'll do it. Ronan, please believe me. I'll pay back every penny if it takes me the rest of my life!'

Ronan's sudden silence, the way he stood over her, looking deep into her eyes, shocked her into stillness, a terrible realisation dawning on her like an icy hand clutching at her nerves.

'It—isn't money, is it?' she managed shakily.

The ferocity with which he shook his dark head left no room for doubt in her reeling thoughts.

'And what hurts is that you ever thought it could be. Did you really believe I was the sort of man who'd act as I did for *money*?'

'No...'

Deep down inside Lily admitted to herself that she'd always known. That she'd never really believed him capable of that, even in the middle of hating him with all her heart. Even then she had never thought that he could really be so petty, so vindictive, so downright cruel.

Swallowing hard, she forced herself to meet the laser-like blaze of his eyes, her chin coming up and her shoulders straightening as she nerved herself to accept what was coming. It wasn't going to be easy, she knew, but it had to be faced.

'I know you didn't tie Davey into the sort of contract he claims you did. Which can only mean that my brother lied to me from the start. So why don't you tell me what really happened, Ronan? Why don't you tell me the truth?'

CHAPTER TWELVE

HE DIDN'T want to tell her.

The realisation set Lily's nerves jangling, pressing the panic button that sent her pulse-rate into overdrive, beating high up in her throat so that she could hardly breathe. What could be so bad that he wanted to protect her from it?

He didn't want to tell her.

The words beat inside Ronan's skull like a pain. Because now it seemed that everything he had feared when lying awake in the darkness of the night had come true, and he didn't know how to live with that truth.

He had believed that Davey had told Lily everything and that, if not actually condoning his crime, she had connived with him to get him away. He had believed that she had tried to buy her brother's safety, and so convinced himself that anything he took from her was justified on her own amoral terms.

But now it seemed that she was innocent of any such thing. She didn't know what Davey had done, and, blinded by the need for revenge, he had taken her life and smashed it, trampling on her feelings with only the faintest protest from his conscience.

So what did that make him? No better than her damn brother, that was for sure. And now she wanted the truth.

And if he told her he knew what would happen. She would hate him more than ever, and with good cause. She would want him out of her life for good, and he would have lost any chance of ever finding out more about the real Lily, the one he had so blindly refused to let himself see when he had started out on this.

But at least he could make things as easy as possible for her. If it could ever be easy for her to find out that she had been used and lied to by both himself and her brother.

And so he insisted that they dressed and had breakfast before they talked. But for both of them it was just a question of going through the motions, neither of them eating much, and obviously grateful for the chance to stop pretending to swallow food they had no appetite for.

At last Ronan took his coffee through into the lounge and Lily followed him silently, torn between wanting to know the whole truth and a cold, sneaking fear of just what she might discover about Davey and Ronan himself.

'You'd best sit down,' Ronan instructed when she hovered in the doorway, unsure of what to do.

'Will I need to?'

She regretted the impulse of flippancy as soon as the words were out. Anyone looking into Ronan's face, seeing the frown that darkened his features, the bleakness of his eyes, would know that levity didn't fit with the mood at all.

'Sorry,' she muttered, plumping herself down in a chair.

Her stomach seemed to be turning somersaults while filled with the frantic fluttering of a thousand butterfly wings, so that she felt distinctly nauseous. The smell of her own coffee sickened her so that she hastily put it aside.

'It's strange how one's life can change in six months,' Ronan began, his tone as sombre and joyless as any judge pronouncing a life sentence. 'Just twenty-four short weeks, and everything you ever believed in or held dear can be destroyed or so irrevocably damaged that there's no possible hope of repair.'

Six months? Lily wondered. It hadn't been even four since she had first meet Ronan. But in those weeks her life had been blasted apart as if in the grip of some violent typhoon.

'I know,' she said feelingly, and at her quiet words Ronan's dark head jerked up, blue-grey eyes blazing into hers.

'Yes, I suppose you do.'

He dropped his gaze to his coffee mug again, staring into it as if he felt as little enthusiasm for the drink as she had done.

'And I suppose my situation was very similar to the one you found yourself in when you were seventeen. Six months ago I would have said that I had almost everything a man could want. I had a thriving business, work that absorbed me, more money than I knew what to do with. I had success, health, but most of all I had a wonderful family.'

Lily's heart kicked sharply in her chest, making her gasp out loud.

'I *had* a family,' he had said. The words tolled inside her head like some terrible death knell for any hopes she had. They were made all the more ominous by the recollection of Ronan's response to her questions about his guests at the wedding.

'No family,' he had said. 'There's no family.' And with a terrible feeling like a knife being twisted in a wound she heard his voice confirm her worst fears.

'I had a father, mother, and a little sister I adored. Now...'

'Oh, God, Ronan! What happened?'

'Your brother happened.' His face changed as he spoke, the sensual mouth twisting bitterly, eyes hard as tempered steel.

'D-Davey?'

'Davey.' The confirmation was cold and harsh. 'Davey bloody Cornwell. Let me tell you about your brother and my family. About what I call the "Cornwell effect".'

No! Lily wanted to cry. She longed to close her ears with her hands, blot out the sound of that appallingly controlled voice. She didn't want to hear the things it would tell her. But she knew she had to go through with this, even if it destroyed her very soul to do so.

'Tell me.' It was just a whisper. But Ronan needed no encouragement. He had already determined on a path and he was going to follow it, no matter what.

'My sister, Rosalie, was just coming up to eighteen and in the final year of her A level courses...'

Rosalie. Lily's nerves tightened even further, recalling that 'Rosalie used to say' which he had cut off so abruptly. She had thought he'd meant some ex-girlfriend, but he had been talking about his sister.

'She was very bright, very beautiful. Here...'

He reached into a pocket and pulled out his wallet. Extracting a photograph, he tossed it onto the table between them so that Lily could see it clearly.

A young girl, tall and slim. Her vivid colouring was Ronan's intensified: bright blue eyes and tumbling auburn hair. Her smile was wide and brilliantly happy, and Lily winced inside at the thought of that 'I *had* a little sister.'

'She had a wonderful future ahead of her. She was going to university. She wanted to be a lawyer, and she would have made it too, but she met your brother.'

His right fist slammed into the palm of his other hand with a violence that made Lily start fearfully, flinching back into her chair.

'*I* introduced her to Davey.'

'Oh, don't!' Lily pleaded, unable to bear the bitterness of self-reproach in his words.

The look Ronan turned on her was blackly sardonic, bitterly mocking in a way that tore at her heart.

'In the pack of lies your brother seems to have told you, there was one bit of the truth. I did put him under contract—but only to rescue him from the mess he'd already got himself into.'

'And why did you do that?' It seemed an impossibly generous thing to do.

Ronan shrugged off her question.

'Davey doesn't have a monopoly on messing things up. When I was nineteen, and in my first year at university, I almost went off the rails. I was having too much fun to work so I skipped lectures, didn't hand in work. It was only when I realised that I had to re-sit my exams or be thrown out that I got my act together. So I knew something of how he felt. And besides, Davey has real talent. He's an amazing musician with the soaring voice of an angel. He's also a brilliant songwriter who could write the most amazing lyrics. He played me a couple of his compositions. They would have made the devil himself weep.'

The words were choked off and for the space of several heartbeats there was a silence so profound that Lily felt it close around her throat, stifling any attempt to speak. She couldn't take her eyes from Ronan, from the pallor of his ravaged face, the anguish that burned in his eyes.

'They made Rosalie weep,' he said rawly.

'Oh, God!'

Lily fought against tears she was afraid to let fall. She feared that Ronan might think they were for Davey, and so misjudge where her sympathies lay. The terrible problem was that she was beginning to feel there was no one person who deserved her tears most. Already her heart was breaking for everyone involved in this story.

Ronan sighed deeply, pushing a rough hand through his hair.

'I knew about Davey's drinking—no one could miss that. What I wasn't aware of was that he had a drugs habit as well.'

'Drugs!'

It was a cry of horror that drew Ronan's haunted eyes to her face.

'You didn't know? But when he was here that time, didn't you even suspect?'

'I...'

She hadn't known, but now that she did it explained so much. Davey's violent mood swings, the frequent changes from wildly frenetic gaiety to total blank apathy when nothing could rouse him. The dull look in his eyes, the loss of weight—the disappearance of money from her purse.

'What...?' Once more she tried to speak, and again her voice failed her. But Ronan interpreted the question she wanted to ask with almost telepathic ease.

'He started on Ecstasy, but I suspect he tried a bit of everything. By the time I met him he was definitely into heroin.'

'Oh, Davey!' How could this have happened to him? To her baby brother?

Unable to stay still a moment longer, she got to her feet and paced restlessly round the room, her hands clenched together before her.

'I never knew he'd gone so completely off the rails.' And, blinded by her love for him, the way she'd always cared for him, she hadn't been able to see it.

Ronan's silent nod was a sombre acknowledgement of the fact that he believed her.

'I tried to deal with the problem—to get him into some sort of programme to sort himself out. I promised him I'd help him to a great future if he was clean. I really believed he could have that future, but I'd reckoned without his so-called friends—the members of a band he used to play in.'

His head swung round to her as Lily drew in her breath in a hiss of alarm.

'Davey was never any good at choosing friends. He wanted so much to be liked and accepted that he'd go along with anything anyone suggested if they'd just be his mates...'

'His partners in crime,' Ronan inserted sardonically. 'They supplied the drink and the drugs and they were totally wrong for him. Lily, your brother had more talent in his little finger than the rest of that crew put together. But under their influence he messed up everything.'

'He told me.'

Seeing the way that Ronan's hand was clenched around his coffee cup, and suddenly fearful that the handle might actually snap under the pressure, Lily moved to try and take it from him. Pausing to look deep into his cobalt blue eyes, she added sincerely, 'He felt very bad about it.'

'He needed to,' was the curt response. Ronan's face was as hard and sculpted as a marble statue. 'I had thought that tying him into a binding contract would bring him to his senses, force him to face reality and work hard for what I knew he could achieve. When he was thrown out of his flat for not paying the rent, I invited him to stay with me for a while, and that was where he met my sister.'

Pushing the mug at her, he got to his feet and strode to the patio doors that led into the garden. For a long, taut moment he stared out at the rain, rejection stamped into every line of his long body so that Lily was afraid he would turn on her if she so much as touched him.

'Rosalie arrived while I was out. By the time I got back it was obvious that Davey had already charmed his way into her heart. He's a good-looking lad, your brother, and when he sets his mind to something there are few people who can resist him.'

Unseen behind that straight, proud back, Lily couldn't suppress a wry smile. She could think of another male who fitted that description only too well.

'But you warned your sister off.'

It was the only thing he could have done. Loving Rosalie as

he did, he wouldn't have wanted her to get mixed up with the sort of loser her brother had become.

'What the hell else do you think I did?'

Ronan swung round to face her again, making her heart clench at the realisation that he had taken her comment totally the wrong way, seeing in it a criticism where none had been intended.

'I wanted her to give me time to get him sorted out, back on the straight and narrow, but she saw my actions as the heavy-handed tyranny of an older brother. Told me I knew nothing about love. I think she saw herself as Juliet and Davey as her Romeo. Certainly, the end result was much the same.'

He pushed both hands through his hair and Lily was upset to see how they shook, revealing the strength of emotion that was otherwise only displayed in the shocking bleakness of his eyes. She longed to go to him, to hold him and comfort him, but knew intuitively that he would reject any such gesture on her part.

'What happened?'

'On her eighteenth birthday Davey took her to a club to celebrate. It was a place he'd been to frequently, somewhere where he knew he could get a fix any time he wanted.'

'Oh, no...' Lily whispered, knowing with a terrible sense of inevitability what was coming.

'Oh, yes!' Ronan snarled viciously. 'He fed her Ecstasy. One single bloody tablet...'

The curses he spat out were savage, darkly eloquent of a pain he wouldn't let his face express. It was as if he had kept the agony inside all this time, where it had festered, growing every day, eating away at him.

'*One tablet!* It killed her. She was on a life-support system for a few days, but deep down we all knew there was no hope.'

Slowly Lily turned back to the coffee table, looking down at the photograph of Rosalie Ronan had left lying there. Tears burned in her eyes at the thought of that lovely, laughing creature lying still and cold, the vivid blue eyes closed, all the vibrant life snuffed out. Recalling how desolate she had felt when her parents had died too early, she felt she could share some of the shock and anguish Ronan had endured with that terrible loss.

'Ronan, I'm so sorry...'

But he hadn't heard her. He was heading out of the room, almost through the door before she realised.

'Ronan!'

Stunned and confused, she stumbled after him, catching him up in the hall.

'Ronan, wait!'

The look he turned on her was like a blow to her face. It was the sort of feeling one might experience after tracking down a wounded leopard, only to have it turn and face its hunter with vicious, snarling defiance. And the fact that she had expected his rejection made it no easier to bear.

'That's not all, is it?'

'Isn't it enough?'

More than enough. More than she could bear. But no matter how much she dreaded it, she had to know the full truth.

Ronan was moving again, getting away from her. She had to force her legs to carry her as she followed him down the hall and out on to the drive. The rain had ceased now, the only sound the slow drip of water from the leaves to the ground.

The scene reminded her agonisingly of that first day after their wedding, when she had trailed after him in much the same way. Then, as now, she had needed an explanation he wasn't prepared to give her.

'Ronan, *tell me!*'

He came to such an abrupt halt that she almost cannoned into him from behind. But when she moved in front of him to see his face her heart quailed at the sight of his ashen pallor, the way it made his eyes look like deep, haunted pools.

'*Tell me!*' she insisted.

His sigh seemed to come from the depths of his soul, and for the space of five uncertain seconds she thought that he would shake his head and refuse to tell her. But then he squared his shoulders, as if accepting the inevitable. His hands were clenched at his sides, revealing the brutal control he was exerting to hold himself still, the effort it took to bring himself to speak.

'My father had to make the decision to have Rosalie's life-support system switched off. It destroyed him. No parent expects to outlive their child. He went into the garage, fed a hosepipe from the exhaust into the car and turned on the engine. I was the one who found him.'

The horror of that moment was gouged into his face, etched in lines so deep that she doubted if anything could ever erase them.

'Was he...?' She couldn't bring herself to complete the question.

'No, thank God. I got to him just in time, but it was touch and go for a while.'

Cold, dark eyes looked into her shocked face with something close to grim satisfaction.

'Well, you asked,' he said with bitter flippancy.

'Yes, I asked.'

And now she knew. Deep inside she felt as if she was breaking apart, as if she would never, ever be whole again.

'And your mother?'

'My mother? She survived—just. She couldn't go under because of my father's despair. He needed her like never before.'

'You told me you had no family.'

'I lied.' It was cold, and final as a knife. 'Well, no, it wasn't exactly a lie. Perhaps I should have told you I had no family who would want to come to the wedding.'

'And of course neither your mother nor your father would fit into that category.'

And now, too, she saw how careful he had been. His wedding guests had not been his family but associates from work, little more than acquaintances, who wouldn't know or talk about his private life. Except for his best man, whose attitude had disturbed her at the time.

'Precisely. After all, I could hardly say, Mum, Dad, I'm marrying the sister of the guy who fed Rosalie the tablet that killed her—want to come?' The black humour burned into Lily's vulnerable heart with the bite of concentrated acid. 'I think they might have been a little reluctant to turn up.'

'You didn't tell them the truth?' The truth was that he had used his marriage to her as a weapon against her brother, nothing more.

A shake of Ronan's dark head declared the idea was impossible.

'They had enough to cope with already. I thought I'd handle things myself.'

'And by ''handle things'' you mean you went all out for vengeance?'

This time his nod was grim-faced, emotionless.

'I wanted to hurt the man responsible, destroy him as he'd destroyed my family. But I couldn't find Davey. He'd gone into hiding as soon as Rosalie was taken into hospital. But I knew there was another way.'

'Me.' She had to force herself to say it.

'You,' Ronan confirmed harshly.

If he could have denied it, he would. But he had promised her the truth, however much it cost him.

And what did it matter now anyway? He had lost her, as he had known he would. It was there in her eyes, in the shadows that darkened them, and in the cool, distant sound of her voice. *Lost her.* He almost laughed out loud at the bitter irony of it. What did he have to lose? Lily had made it only too plain how she felt. She had spelled it out to him no more than a week ago. He might be able to touch her body, to bring it to quivering, demanding life beneath his hands, but he had never been able to reach her mind, which was totally closed against him. She hated him for what he had done, and who could blame her? Right now he detested himself.

'Davey had talked of you often. What you did, where you lived. I thought that if I couldn't get to him in any other way I could do it through you. I looked on it as poetic justice. Not an eye for an eye, but a sister for a sister. That way I could wander into your life as carelessly as Davey had done into Rosalie's...'

'And destroy my happiness? Destroy me?'

At least he had the grace not to dodge the question. He looked her right in the eyes as he answered.

'Yes. That was what I planned.'

'And are you happy now?'

'Happy?' Ronan echoed as if he hadn't understood the word.

'No, to tell you the truth, I'm not. Happiness doesn't come into it.'

'You're not? Well, what *will* make you happy?'

She flung the word at him in a mixture of pain, defiance and sheer horror at the thought that even now he still wasn't satisfied. What Davey had done was terrible, but he at least had the conscience to feel bad, to be racked with guilt about what he had done.

'What will it take to put an end to this twisted campaign of hatred of yours? When you've completely destroyed my life? Because you have! When you've made me hate you more than any other human being on earth? When you've...'

With each accusation she took a step forward, towards him, and found to her astonishment that Ronan was actually backing away from her, his hands coming up as if in defence against her.

The idea that Ronan might need protection in any form from her was so preposterous that it almost burned away the anguish she was feeling. Almost but not quite.

'When were you going to get out of my life, Ronan? When were you going to go and leave me in peace for good? Just how far were you prepared to go, I wonder? Was it Davey you wanted to destroy completely, or did you want to see me dead, like Rosalie?'

That stopped him, freezing him in his tracks as he stared at her, every trace of colour leaching from his face.

'God, Lily, *no*! Never that! I never thought...'

'You *never thought* at all!' Bitterly she echoed his own fraught words. 'You never thought to tell me what Davey had done, to give me a chance to show you that I felt as badly about it as you could ever do. You never thought to find out what I would have done...'

'You couldn't—'

'I couldn't have done anything? Did you even give me a chance? I would have done *anything*, anything at all to put it right!'

'*Anything?*' It had an odd intonation, as if he couldn't quite get his tongue round the word. 'You care for your brother that much?'

'I love my brother every bit as much as you ever loved your sister. There, does that answer your question?'

It did, but there was no way he liked what he'd heard. If he'd ever wondered why she had ended up in bed with him after saying she'd rather die, then now he knew.

'You have to let me help my brother!' she had said. And he had come back at her with the declaration that he knew how loving someone with all your heart could drive you to do something desperate, something that in a more rational frame of mind you would never even consider.

And Lily had done just that. She had offered herself up as a sacrifice for Davey's sake, believing it might help his cause. She had slept with him because she thought it might go some way towards appeasing the anger he felt towards her brother.

There was no way back now. No chance of ever healing the wounds he had inflicted on her. He had done too much to hurt her, so that now the only thing he could do was to do exactly as she asked and leave her in peace.

It struck home with the blackest, most bitter of ironies that in the same moment he had actually realised he loved this woman, he also knew that the only way he could prove it was by turning and walking away from her.

'Yes.' He forced the reply past lips that seemed so stiff he might almost believe they were carved from wood. 'I think that answers my question perfectly. And so now I'll give you the answer to yours.'

'My...?' Lily tried to make herself think, remember what she had asked. But her brain wouldn't function. It seemed to have turned to ice, like the blood in her veins, frozen by the wintry tone, the glacial disdain in his eyes.

'You asked when I was going to get out of your life—go and leave you in peace for good, was the exact phrase you used.'

'But...'

She couldn't force her tongue to form the words to tell him that she had only spoken in anger and in pain. That the last thing she wanted was for him to go out of her life. That she loved him and she would die if he left her again.

But to do so would be worse than useless, not to mention

totally unfair. Ronan didn't love her. He had only seen her as the instrument of his revenge against Davey, nothing more.

And what Davey had done would always come between them. Her brother had hurt Ronan and his family so badly that she couldn't bring herself to add to that distress by putting pressure on him to maintain links with the family he so detested.

She loved Ronan more than life itself, but she knew with a terrible irony that she could only show that love by letting him go, by setting him free to find someone else in the future, someone who might help him heal the scars of the loss of his sister.

And so she stood silent, listening without saying a word, though her heart cried out an anguished protest as Ronan continued.

'The answer is that I'm leaving now. Just as soon as I can pack I'll be out of your life and you needn't worry that I'll ever come back. This time I really will leave you in peace for good. In fact, I'll do more than that. I'll set you free. The minute I get back to London I'll get my solicitor to start work on the divorce papers.'

CHAPTER THIRTEEN

AUTUMN was definitely on its way, Lily reflected sadly as she stared out of the window, not really seeing the view before her. The warmth of the summer had lasted right through September, but now the nights were drawing in so much more quickly, and there was a distinct chill in the air.

The garden which had been her salvation when Ronan had left, keeping her mind busy and tiring her physically so that at least she had a chance of sleep, was now faded and drab and preparing for the onset of winter. The leaves on the trees were already beginning to fall.

'Stop it!' she reproved herself, swinging away from the depressing sight. 'Stop reckoning everything from the date when Ronan left!'

It only emphasised the fact that he had gone, and how, true to his word, he clearly meant to stay away, never even contacting her. It forced her to confront the huge, gaping hole in her life and in her heart, stabbing at her afresh with the anguish of her loss, the months of heartbreak she had endured.

But then it was difficult *not* to do so, she thought wryly as her eyes were caught by the way that her movement was reflected in the mirror on the opposite wall.

A faint smile curved her lips as she considered the image of herself that she could see there, absently smoothing the blue material of her dress over the gentle swelling of her abdomen that declared her condition to the world.

Obviously she had to date her pregnancy from the time when Ronan had been with her during the summer. She had probably conceived her baby during that first passionate night they had spent together after the trip to Leeds, when they had both been so hungry, so desperate for each other, that they hadn't paused to consider such practical matters as protection.

Certainly she had first been made aware of it by the way that the nausea she had taken as a nervous response to the stress of Ronan's departure had lingered persistently until it had finally become evident that it was more than that. A hurried check on dates had left her with only one possible conclusion.

The sound of the doorbell jolted her out of her melancholy reverie and sent her hurrying across the hall.

For a couple of blank, confused seconds she didn't recognise the young man who stood on the doorstep. He looked familiar, and yet...

But then he grinned widely, and suddenly realisation dawned with a sense of shock.

'Hello, big sister. Surprised to see me?' It had an edge of embarrassed, almost defiant uncertainty to it, as if he was unsure as to what sort of reception he would receive.

'Davey!'

Beside herself with delight, Lily enfolded him in an ecstatic hug.

'Where have you been? Why didn't you get in touch? One letter in all this time...'

'Yeah, I know. I'm sorry about that.' Davey eased himself out of her embrace looking decidedly shamefaced. 'I wanted to let you know I was OK but there was something I had to do. I needed to get my act together...'

'It looks as if you've managed that.'

Lily's voice was shaken as she fully took in the change in her brother for the first time. This was a new Davey, bright-eyed, clear-skinned, with the glow of good health about him.

His fair hair was as long as ever, but it shone with the effects of regular care, and although his clothes were the usual tee shirt and jeans they were clean and new, and it was evident that he took a pride in his appearance. He had filled out a bit too, as if he had had more than a few square meals since he'd left.

'What happened to you?'

'Ronan Guerin—no...'

Davey had caught the flash of apprehension in her eyes and hurried to reassure her.

'He didn't do anything to harm me, Lill. On the contrary, he was the one who picked me up and got me sorted out—put me through detox, got me into therapy. That's where I've been all this time...'

'Ronan did?' But then something else Davey had said pulled at her thoughts. 'Detox? You're...?'

'I'm clean, Lill. Clean and sober, and I plan on staying that way. It wasn't easy. If you must know, at times it was hell on earth, but Ronan stuck by me, supported me every step of the way. And now I'm out the other side I have no intention of ever going back. I was badly screwed up, Sis, and I made some terrible mistakes.'

'Rosalie,' Lily murmured, and at the sound of the name her brother's eyes darkened.

'Rosalie,' he confirmed, his voice low, his eyes on the ground. 'Ronan said he'd told you.'

Suddenly he looked up again, catching hold of Lily's hand.

'But I want you to know something important, Sis. I wasn't the one who gave Rosalie that tablet; I swear I wasn't! I was there, of course, but I was too phased out to know what was happening, and one of the other guys persuaded her to try it.'

His hands clenched on hers, the glimmer of tears in his eyes.

'But I *felt* responsible. If only *I'd* been more in control. If I hadn't been so bloody out of my head myself I would have been able to stop it, or at least take action sooner when I realised she was in distress. I'll never forgive myself for that, Lill. I loved that girl; I really did.'

'Does Ronan know this?'

The question came rather breathlessly. Her heart had leapt into a swift, shallow patter at the thought that if Ronan learned that Davey hadn't been responsible for Rosalie's death, as he had thought, then maybe, just maybe, there might be a chance for them.

'He knows.' Davey was unaware of the way that his answer took that one last trace of hope from her. 'When I finally got up the nerve to go and tell him the truth I found that he was prepared to meet me more than halfway. We talked for hours, all about when I was a kid and the way that Mum and Dad died. That was when he arranged for me to go into this programme. He saved my life, Lily.'

'Oh, Davey, you don't know how much this means to me.'

Taking her brother by the hand, Lily drew him inside, using the action to disguise the way that hot tears were burning in her eyes. Ronan could find it in his heart to forgive Davey for what had happened, but he couldn't bring himself to contact her.

'He insisted that I write to you, to let you know I was all right, and that as soon as I got out I came to see you. And if I stay clean he's going to help me have the sort of career I've always dreamed of. And I *will* stay clean, Sis. I'll do it for Rosalie, and for you and Ronan.'

Lily could only manage a wordless sound in response to the way her name and Ronan's had been so unknowingly yoked together.

'I have to admit that I'm scared. It's one hell of a responsibility, but with Ronan's backing I know that I can do it. I owe him so much.'

Ronan was there for Davey, Lily thought bitterly, but not for her. Their fake marriage had turned into a real, lifelong commitment for her, but to Ronan it still meant nothing at all.

'You look different, Lill.' Davey had finally noticed the change in her appearance. 'What's changed—? You're pregnant!'

'Four—nearly five months,' Lily confirmed, her voice a blend of shaken laughter and the close threat of tears. It was impossible not to see in the delighted grin that spread across her brother's face the response that Ronan might have shown to the news if only things had been so very different.

'Is it Ronan's?' Davey stunned her by asking. 'He said you'd had a bit of a thing together.'

A *bit of a thing*. Lily swallowed down a choking cry as she nodded miserably. The derogatory description shattered her self-control; the tears would no longer be held back and spilled over, streaming down her cheeks.

'Oh, Lill! Does he know?'

'I—I haven't told him.'

'You haven't...? But, Lill, you *have to*! He's got a right to know about his child. And can't you see how important it is?

It's something good—something positive to come out of all of this.'

Lily doubted that Ronan would see it that way.

'He wouldn't want it, Davey,' she choked out. 'He hates our family.'

But even as she spoke she picked out the flaw in her own words. If Ronan truly hated them so much, then he would never have helped her brother as he had.

'He doesn't love me,' she amended painfully.

'Are you so sure of that?' Davey asked sharply. 'Lily, the Ronan I've been with these past months isn't the same man I knew before. He's changed. It's as if a light's gone out inside him, and it's not only because of Rosalie. He's like someone who's just going through the motions of living, but doesn't really give a damn about anything. I couldn't understand what was behind it, but now I could hazard a guess.'

He saw the light dawn in his sister's eyes, the small, tentative flame of hope she couldn't extinguish.

'You have to go to him—tell him.'

'I can't!' It was a despairing whisper. 'What if he shuts the door in my face? It would kill me if that happened—especially now.'

'You'll never know until you try. I know he'll never come here. He told me you wanted him out of your life and that the only thing he could do for you was stay away.'

'He said *that*?' Lily's head came up sharply. 'The only thing he could *do for me*?'

She couldn't help it. Deep inside a tiny seed of longing had taken root and was starting to grow. Was it possible? Could it be true that Ronan felt something for her?

Davey was right; there was only one way she would ever find out. But did she have the courage to go through with it?

Ronan's elegant London home was dark and shuttered when Lily reached it the next day, tipping her mood from nervous apprehension into black despair.

Please don't let him be away, she prayed silently. Please let him be here!

But her ring at the doorbell met with no response, and the windows remained dark and empty, with no sign of life.

So what did she do now? She could wait, but who knew if Ronan would even come back home tonight? What if Davey had got it all wrong? What if, far from hating life alone, he was in fact revelling in his freedom, thankful that his solicitor had the matter of the divorce in hand?

The *divorce*. That thought stopped her dead, stilling her feet when she would have turned away, admitting defeat. Ronan had threatened divorce as soon as possible. He had said that he would put the matter straight into his solicitor's hands. Why, then, hadn't she heard anything?

It was then that the faint gleam caught her eye. It was just a hint of light, somewhere at the back of the house, spilling out into the garden through a window or a glass door. Moving cautiously, Lily made her way towards it.

After edging her way along a path by the side of the house, she found that a large sitting room looked out over the enormous garden, with glass patio doors running almost the whole width of one wall. The room itself was in darkness, except for the glow of a real coal fire set in the marble hearth. Ronan must have lit it against the chill of the evening, she thought, gathering her coat closer round her. It really was quite cold tonight.

But at least that meant that wherever he had gone he was planning to come back before long. She was just turning away when a slight movement caught her attention, freezing her where she stood.

'Ronan!'

The name escaped her in a whisper as she saw the man stretched out on the settee, so obviously deeply asleep that even her tentative ring at the doorbell hadn't woken him. Peering through the glass, she could just make out the long-limbed masculine form, the strongly carved face, the dark hair dimly illuminated by the flickering light of the fire.

Her hand was already raised to rap on the glass when she changed her mind. She couldn't just intrude on him like that, startling him awake. She could just imagine how he would feel, jolted from sleep to find the 'wife' he had thought he'd left well behind peering in at him.

But what could she do? As she pushed her hands deep into her coat pockets her fingers touched the cold hardness of metal. The keys that Davey had given her.

'Ronan told me to use his house as my own,' her brother had told her. 'That's why he gave me his keys. Take them with you; you never know, they might come in handy.'

Her heart racing fearfully, Lily hurried back to the front of the house and inserted the key in the lock. Turning it cautiously, so as to make as little sound as possible, she opened the door and crept into the large hallway.

She was barely inside before every one of her senses went on red alert. Something was wrong, very wrong; instinctively she sensed it.

Glancing round nervously, she sniffed the air like a nervous cat. *Burning!* All the tiny hairs on the back of her neck lifted in panic. Something was burning close at hand.

Moving swiftly, she crossed to the door she believed led to the room she had seen from outside and pushed it open. The smell was worse now, and drifts of smoke were already clouding the room. As she froze in horror the fire spat again, and a second glowing coal landed on the rug beside the first, flaring into flame as it caught the edge of a discarded newspaper.

The flames licked greedily at the paper, growing brighter, moving steadily, creeping towards...

'*Ronan!*'

With a cry she launched herself forward, grabbing a cushion as she went. Frantically she beat at the flames with her improvised extinguisher, heedless of the way they curled up around its edges, catching her hands. She didn't stop until she was sure that they were all out, continuing long after the last one had finally died.

On the settee, Ronan moved restlessly, disturbed by the noise. Heavy eyelids flickered open and he stared in disbelief at the scene before him.

Lily, here? No, it couldn't be true. He had to be still asleep and dreaming, as he so often did, that she had come back into

his life. But he always woke to find that once more his imagi-
nation had been playing cruel tricks on him. As it was doing
now.

Blinking hard, he focused again, and found that the blonde-
haired woman was still there.

'What…? Lily?'

From behind her Lily heard Ronan's voice. He sounded dazed,
confused, and still only half-awake.

'Lily…for God's sake, Lily, it's out!'

Firm hands closed over her arms, stilling their panicked move-
ments.

'It's *out*!' he repeated more emphatically, the phrase laced
with undertones she couldn't begin to interpret.

'Oh—yes…'

Her own voice came and went like a badly tuned radio, finally
failing her completely as he hauled her to her feet and held her
close just for a moment.

But she was released almost immediately, Ronan leaving her
side to cross the room. The light was switched on, and when he
turned to face her she was shocked by the change in his appearance.

Dressed in a black sweatshirt and jeans, he had obviously lost
weight, and there were deep shadows under the blue eyes. He
looked haggard and drawn, as if from loss of sleep. His evident
exhaustion was clearly the reason why he hadn't sensed the fire
before she had.

Was it possible that she was the cause of this? Had Davey
been right when he had told her that he thought Ronan was
missing her?

'God, Lily, your hands!'

Ronan's shocked exclamation had her looking down, staring
in blank incomprehension at the red marks on her palms and
wrists.

'You're hurt! You must have burned yourself.'

'I—I hadn't realised.'

It was true. She hadn't felt any pain, or even thought about
herself. Her only concern had been to save Ronan.

'You—' Ronan broke off sharply, swallowing down what he had been about to say. 'Let me look.'

Lifting her hands, he touched the injured palms with gentle fingers, his strong-featured face absorbed.

'This one needs a dressing on it. Come into the kitchen. There's a first-aid kit in there.'

Lily followed obediently, submitting to his ministrations in silence. She wouldn't have been able to speak if she'd tried. His concern, his care was almost too much for her to bear.

'I'm not sure that I shouldn't take you to the hospital.' Ronan had caught the glimmer of tears in her eyes and mistaken the reason for them. 'Are you in a lot of pain?'

Compared with the emotional distress she felt, any physical discomfort was negligible, but she couldn't tell him that. Not when in spite of the concern and attention he had shown her he had spoken no word of affection, revealed no sign of being glad that she was there.

'No, there's no need for that, really.'

Besides, how could she say the things she'd come here to tell him in the impersonal, clinical surroundings of a hospital accident unit?

'This will be fine, honest.' She brandished her hand to display the bandage he'd applied.

But the careful bravado of the gesture was ruined when a sudden wave of dizziness assailed her, making her sway on her feet and press her fingers against her temples.

'Lily...'

His hands went out to her, but she pulled away sharply. The urge to sink into his embrace, to surrender completely to the need to be held was almost overwhelming but she couldn't give in to it. Ronan was kind and attentive, but that was all. He would do the same for anyone who was hurt. It wasn't evidence of any stronger feeling for her alone.

'It's just a reaction. If I could sit down...'

'Of course.'

He led her back into the sitting-room, which Lily now saw was decorated in shades of rust and cream, and settled her on the terracotta-coloured settee.

'If the fire bothers you, I could...'

'No,' she reassured him hastily. 'It's fine.'

And it was. The flames leaping in the grate no longer troubled her. She had faced her fear of fire and overcome it; if only she could do the same where Ronan was concerned. But there she had so much to lose that she didn't dare take the risk of tackling it head-on.

Ronan came to sit in the chair opposite her, leaning towards her, his arms resting on his knees. His eyes were dark and intent as they fixed on her face.

'Lily, just why are you here? What brought you to London?'

Frantically Lily hunted for some sort of answer that wouldn't give too much away.

'It's about this marriage of ours,' she managed at last. 'We can't go on this way any longer.'

'I see.'

Ronan sat back abruptly, feeling as if something had struck him hard. He could feel the blood draining from his face, taking with it every trace of the hope he had foolishly allowed himself to let into his mind.

Holding back on the divorce had been his final gamble. He had let himself believe that if he dragged his feet on that, if he delayed putting it in the hands of his solicitors, then Lily might just reconsider. She might come round to forgiving him for the appalling things he'd done and be prepared to give him a chance to make their parody of a marriage into a real one.

But it had been a long shot, and it seemed that it had failed.

'Of course.' His voice was low and flat, no emotion in it. 'I wondered when this would happen. Who is he?'

'Who is who?' Lily couldn't follow his logic.

'The other guy. The one you want to be with. I take it you've come to find out why I've been so slow about arranging the divorce.'

'I've come about no such thing!' The words escaped her before she had a chance to consider whether they were wise. She only knew that she couldn't let Ronan believe there was any other man in her life.

Something raw and unconcealed flared in his eyes.

'Then why *are* you here?'

The moment had come, but at the thought of actually revealing what was in her heart panic, sharp and searing, raced through her veins. From being shiveringly cold she was now burning hot, in a way that was not just the effect of the fire.

With a shaking hand she brushed the beads of sweat from her forehead, then wished she hadn't as she saw Ronan's vigilant gaze follow the slight movement.

'Don't you think you'd be more comfortable if you took off your coat?'

Lily knew she had no choice but to do as he suggested. To refuse would only be to alert his suspicions, make him wonder just what she had to conceal.

Drawing a deep breath, she stood up slowly and slipped off the navy raincoat that had concealed her shape until now.

He saw the change in her at once. Far more quickly than Davey had done. But then he was much more intimately acquainted with her body than her brother had ever been. And only now did she realise how the rose-coloured floral print of her dress matched exactly the shade of the silk shift she had worn on that momentous night when he had taken her to the club in Leeds. The night when she believed their child had been conceived.

'You're pregnant!'

Ronan's obvious amazement pushed a small, shaken laugh from Lily's lips.

'I could hardly deny it, could I?'

Her hands smoothed the soft jersey material over the small bump that was just beginning to show.

But when she looked into Ronan's face she was shocked to see the fury that blazed in the depths of his eyes, hardening his features until they looked as if they were carved from granite. Had she misjudged everything? Had she got it all wrong—terribly wrong?

'Were you ever going to tell me?' Ronan demanded, his voice as cold and harsh as his expression as he got to his feet in a rush.

'I'm here, aren't I?' Lily returned shakily.

She wished he hadn't stood up. Standing so close to her like this, he seemed to tower over her, his height and strength ominously threatening for all that he hadn't touched her. She felt as if the ground was crumbling away beneath her feet, not knowing whether his anger was because she hadn't told him or because she was pregnant with a child he didn't want.

'It took you long enough!'

'I was—'

'You were...? Lily...?' Ronan pressed ruthlessly when she couldn't bring herself to finish. 'You were what?'

'I was scared!' Pushed over the edge of her control, she flung the word into his face in a mixture of fear and defiance.

'Scared!' he echoed on a note of disbelief. 'Scared of what? That I'd want you to have an abortion? Oh, Lily...'

Abruptly his mood changed, the tension that had held his strong body taut easing, as did the hard lines into which his expression was set.

'You couldn't be more wrong,' he said, so softly that Lily could only stare in confusion and disbelief. 'But you must see that this changes everything. I'm sorry, but you'll have to tell your boyfriend that he's going to have to find someone else. There's no way I'll agree to a divorce now. I—'

'There isn't any boyfriend!' Lily broke in desperately. 'And how many times do I have to tell you that I didn't come here for a divorce?'

'You didn't?' She had his full attention now. 'Then why...?'

Lily had used up all her strength and she sat down rather suddenly, her legs refusing to support her any more. This was it. The next few minutes would decide her future one way or another, make it heaven or hell, depending on the way Ronan reacted to what she had to say.

'Lily!' Ronan came down beside her on the settee. 'Answer the question!'

'You've been doing all the asking so far,' Lily managed unevenly, searching for encouragement, for something on which to pin her hopes in his face.

She didn't know if the flames in the dark pools of his eyes were what she was looking for, only that she couldn't go back now. She had come too far for that. It was time to risk everything on one last throw of the dice.

'It's time you answered a few questions instead. And you can start with telling me why you helped Davey.'

'You've seen him?' It was quick, sharp, and, she was surprised to discover, strangely defensive.

'I've seen him. And I know what you did for him—what you're still doing. But what I want to know, Ronan, is *why*.'

'He didn't give Rosalie that tablet.' His response was a low growl, and he avoided her searching gaze, staring down at where the burning coals had scarred the carpet.

'I know that now. But what surprises me is the fact that you even gave him a chance to explain, and that you believed him when he did. I thought you'd have been more likely to kill him on sight.'

Hot colour washed over Ronan's carved cheekbones as he shook his head fervently.

'The foul way I behaved towards you—the appalling effect it had—cured me of the need for vengeance. I realised it solved nothing, served no purpose at all. It only piled pain on pain and destroyed me as I hurt you.'

Lily's heart leapt at his words, the low-toned voice in which they were spoken seeming to confirm her hope that something good might come of this after all. But still she had to be sure.

'So why...?'

'Why did I help your brother?'

Ronan sighed deeply, long fingers tapping restlessly on the arm of the settee. Or was it nerves that created that jittery movement? Lily found it impossible to judge his mood.

'For his sake. Once you'd told me the story of the way your parents died I knew I could never look at Davey in the same way again. I actually found myself feeling sympathy for him, and when he came to see me, to tell me the truth about what had happened, I saw not the wild, irresponsible thug I'd believed him to be but the real Davey, behind all the bravado, the loss of control. I saw the little boy lost who had been so afraid he might have been responsible for what happened to his mother and father. Who was so scarred by it that he took the blame for

Rosalie's death too, even though he wasn't directly involved. That's one hell of a burden for a kid to carry through life.'

The restless movement of his fingers stopped as Ronan drew in another deep, uneven breath.

'I did it for Rosalie too. She really cared for Davey, after all, and the only thing I could do for her was to make sure he was OK. And, yes, I did it for myself—because after the mess I made of everything else I wanted to put something back, something positive.'

For Davey. For Rosalie. Even for Ronan himself, Lily thought despondently. But had he done any of it for her?

'So I didn't come into it at all,' she said, her voice low and sad.

Ronan's dark head came up sharply, blue-grey eyes blazing into her shadowed amber ones.

'Come into it! Lily, you were *all* of it! You were the only reason for everything. The driving force behind anything I did. I did it all because of you—for you.'

'I...'

But she couldn't speak. It was unbelievable, impossible. Too much to take in all at once. Ronan reached out and took her hands in his.

'I felt so guilty about the appalling way I treated you. I was so cruel, so selfish, so stupidly eaten up by the need I thought I had for vengeance.'

'You were hurting so badly,' Lily put in, unable to bear the anguished self-reproach in his voice. Ronan's vehement shake of his head denied her attempt to justify his actions.

'That's no excuse. In spite of everything that had happened, what I did was wrong, and two wrongs don't make a right. You were innocent and I hurt you terribly. I behaved like a brute. I treated you in a way no human being should ever treat another, let alone—'

He caught himself up sharply, cutting off the end of the sentence, and when he continued it was on a different topic entirely.

'There's something I want you to know. I never meant to make love to you—ever. I fully intended to leave that first night, to go without consummating the marriage so that you could dissolve it easily.'

His smile was wry, self-deprecatory.

'I was going to tell you when we'd eaten, but during that meal you started feeding me and I couldn't stop myself...'

The strong body was shaken by a shudder of sensual remembrance.

'I was lost then, but I couldn't see it. But I never meant things to go that far, and once they had it all became so much more complicated than I had ever imagined. I'm not surprised you hate me so.'

'I don't hate you.' It was soft but confidently spoken.

'But you must.' Ronan looked stunned, his eyes deeply shadowed with confusion. 'I hate myself. I can never forgive all that I...'

'But I can,' Lily put in quietly.

It stopped him dead, his head going back sharply. He looked deep into her eyes, his own dark and bruised, revealing a vulnerability that stabbed straight to her heart.

'You...'

'I can forgive everything you've done.'

'But how?'

'I understand why you behaved as you did. You were hurting and you were lost and confused. And when you love someone it's easy to forgive.'

'Love?'

It was a raw croak, the lack of his normally ruthless control revealing the true depths of his feelings.

'You can't love me! And yet you braved the fire...' he went on, almost to himself, his voice filled with a kind of awe. 'If you knew how I felt when I woke up and saw you. Knowing how terrified of flames you are...'

Lily's smile was wide, gentle, radiant with everything that was in her heart.

'I didn't think about the fire because you were in danger and— because I love you. Oh, Ronan, I do! That's why I'm here. To tell you that I love you and that I want us to start again. I want our marriage to be a real one, our child to have...'

'But you said you hated me!'

'Oh, Ronan!'

Torn between laughter and tears, Lily could only shake her head in dismissal of her own foolish words.

'You don't have the monopoly on saying stupid, hurtful things to hide the pain you're feeling inside. I only said that to conceal how much I really care for you, just as I only let you go because I thought it was one thing I could do for you. Your family had been hurt so much...'

'But I only went because it was the one thing *I* could do for you.'

As Ronan shook his head in despair at his own foolishness, Lily plucked up enough courage to ask the question she most wanted answered.

'Do you think you could finish your sentence now?'

'Finish?' He looked at her with blank incomprehension in his eyes.

'You said that you should never have treated anyone that way, let alone...'

'Let alone the person I love most in all the world,' Ronan completed for her, his voice rich and deep with sincerity. 'And I do, Lily. I love you more than life itself. If you can truly forgive me I'll spend the rest of my time trying to make you happy. I'll—'

He broke off as Lily laid a gentle hand over his mouth to silence him.

'I know,' she said softly. 'I can't help but know. I've seen how much you loved Rosalie. If you give me that sort of devotion, how can I be anything but happy?'

'Oh, Lily...'

She was caught up in his arms, held so tightly it was difficult to breathe. His mouth came down on hers in an ardent, passionate, hungry kiss that communicated his love and need for her far more eloquently than words could ever do.

When he finally released her, her heart was racing, her whole body on fire, the yearning ache that had started up inside her clamouring for appeasement. But there was one more question she had to ask.

'Do you think your parents will be able to accept me...?'

It was Ronan's turn to stop her words with a silencing finger.

'They'll only have to look at you to love you as I do. Lily,' he went on, when her concern still showed on her face. 'They know that Davey wasn't responsible for what happened to Rosalie. And when they find out about the baby they'll be overjoyed to welcome you into the family. Our child will never take my sister's place, but he or she will give my parents someone to love, to help fill the space she left behind. As my wife...'

'Your wife!' Lily echoed the words on a note of awe. It didn't seem possible that she could be Ronan's wife but this time for real, that their marriage could be a proper one.

It was as she lifted a loving hand to touch his face that she remembered and regretted her wild, foolish gesture outside the club in Leeds, when she had flung her ring into the canal.

'Ronan!' It was a cry of distress. 'I don't have a ring! I...'

'I'll give you another one,' Ronan soothed. 'A real wedding ring, one given with love in a true marriage of minds and hearts, not as it was before. We'll have another wedding ceremony too—just the two of us, perhaps with my parents and Davey. And when I promise to love and cherish you, this time you'll know that I mean it.'

Once more she was caught up in his arms and kissed until her senses whirled. And this time the fires that lit inside her could not be subjected to any form of control. This time they raged through her, making her shudder in urgent need against the hard wall of his chest.

'That marriage...' she muttered underneath the heated demand of his mouth. 'The one with hearts and minds—you forgot something.'

'And what was that?' The husky laughter that threaded through the words told her he knew only too well what she meant, but he still wanted her to say it.

Her fingers slid under the hem of his sweatshirt, a wicked smile curving her lips as she felt his uncontrolled reaction, the tensing of strong muscles, the shiver of response.

'You didn't mention bodies. Hearts and minds and *bodies*. An emotional, intellectual and very physical union. That's the sort of marriage I want.'

'Me too,' Ronan agreed, his voice raw with a need that mirrored the one she was feeling. 'I want that sort of marriage too. Would you like me to show you how much?'

The smile Lily shone up straight into his burning eyes was positively beatific in its unconcealed happiness.

'I thought you'd never ask!' she sighed. 'And, yes, I'd like that very, *very* much!'

And as Ronan swung her up into his arms and carried her out of the room her greatest happiness came from knowing that this time she would be his wife not just for a single day but for ever after. For all the days of the rest of their lives.

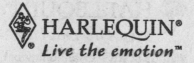

Harlequin Books presents the first title in Carly Phillips' sizzling *Simply* trilogy.

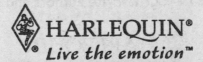

The world's bestselling romance series.

Seduction and Passion Guaranteed!

They're guaranteed to raise your pulse!

Meet the most eligible medical men of the world, in a new series of stories, by popular authors, that will make your heart race!

Whether they're saving lives or dealing with desire, our doctors have got bedside manners that send temperatures soaring....

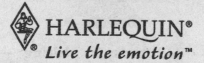

It's romantic comedy with a kick
(in a pair of strappy pink heels)!

Introducing

HARLEQUIN®
flipside™

"It's chick-lit with the romance and happily-ever-after ending that Harlequin is known for."
—*USA TODAY* bestselling author Millie Criswell, author of *Staying Single*, October 2003

"Even though our heroine may take a few false steps while finding her way, she does it with wit and humor."
—Dorien Kelly, author of *Do-Over*, November 2003

Launching October 2003.
Make sure you pick one up!

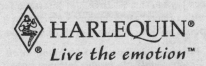

HARLEQUIN®
Live the emotion™

Visit us at www.harlequinflipside.com

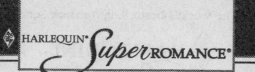

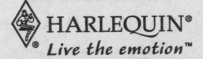